CANYON'S LAST STAND

Canyon O'Grady wasn't trained to be a soldier.
But now he wore the uniform of one. And four
desperate troopers looked to him to tell them
what to do.

"One man to the rear and reload!" Canyon
bellowed. That bought them time, until more
Comanches came at them. Canyon pulled the
men back to the edge of the river and all
reloaded. But they were trapped against the rain-
swollen Brazos.

"Get ready," Canyon called to the four
troopers. He had seen one take an arrow in the
arm and one had been shot in the thigh, but all
were still fighting. "They won't leave us here
long."

He was right. The main force of Comanches
charged. And then it was past time to talk.
There was just time to pray fast . . . and shoot
straight. . . .

CANYON O'GRADY RIDES ON

CANYON O'GRADY

11

SOLDIER'S SONG

by

Jon Sharpe

A SIGNET BOOK

SIGNET
Published by the Penguin Group
Penguin Books USA Inc., 375 Hudson Street,
New York, New York 10014, U.S.A.
Penguin Books Ltd, 27 Wrights Lane,
London W8 5TZ, England
Penguin Books Australia Ltd, Ringwood,
Victoria, Australia
Penguin Books Canada Ltd, 2801 John Street,
Markham, Ontario, Canada L3R 1B4
Penguin Books (N.Z.) Ltd, 182-190 Wairau Road,
Auckland 10, New Zealand

Penguin Books Ltd, Registered Offices:
Hramondsworth, Middlesex, England

First published by Signet, an imprint of New American Library, a division of
Penguin Books USA Inc.

First Printing, January, 1991
10 9 8 7 6 5 4 3 2 1

The first chapter of this book previously appeared in *The Great Land Swindle*,
the tenth volume of this series.

 REGISTERED TRADEMARK—MARCA REGISTRADA

Printed in the United States of America

PUBLISHER'S NOTE
This is a work of fiction. Names, characters, places, and incidents either are
the product of the author's imagination or are used fictitiously, and any resem-
blance to actual persons, living or dead, events, or locales is entirely coinci-
dental.

Canyon O'Grady

His was a heritage of blackguards and poets, fighters and lovers, men who could draw a pistol and bed a lass with the same ease.

Freedom was a cry seared into Canyon O'Grady, justice a banner of his heart.

With the great wave of those who fled to America, the new land of hope and heartbreak, solace and savagery, he came to ride the untamed wildness of the Old West.

With a smile or a six-gun, Canyon O'Grady became a name feared by some and welcomed by others, but remembered by all . . .

*West Texas, 1860 . . .
a place where "savage"
describes more than just
some men's opinions
of the Comanche . . .*

1

Canyon O'Grady stared at the dry earth of west Texas and the obvious trail left by a large group of horses, among them the skid marks of more than a dozen travois. The clearest prints to the outside of the track were plainly from unshod Indian ponies.

"They don't know we're back here yet, Colonel." Company D's advance scout spoke to Canyon's left, addressing Colonel James Henry Colton, commander of Fort Johnson. O'Grady, Johnson, and two companies of the Fourth Cavalry had been tracking the Comanche now for hours. "They're setting up a day camp in the brush about five miles ahead along the Brazos River. Looks like they plan on staying awhile."

Colton waved the scout away, then looked at Canyon, who sat astride his magnificent palomino stallion. "We've got the bastards now," Colton said. "We'll wait for an hour to allow them to settle in and relax. Then we'll hit them from both sides an hour before dark."

"Sounds good," Canyon said. "I'll be glad to lead one of the attacks."

"Hell, no. I need you with me. I want a good evaluation in those reports you take back to Washington." Both men laughed, but both also knew it was the truth.

The Fourth had been ordered out to put an end to a series of raids by Comanche upon west Texas settlements, no matter what it took. So the Fourth Cavalry rode a lot of patrols. This force had come out quickly when scouts had found fresh tracks of a move. *Colonel* Canyon O'Grady rode along as an observer.

Canyon still wasn't used to the attention he received as a "colonel" attached to the inspector general's office in Washington D.C, but the role allowed him to visit Fort Johnson without arousing suspicion. Officers from the IG office regularly inspected forts and evaluated procedures, the abilities of officers and men.

Before Canyon left Washington he had been fitted with a uniform, given a spare, and taken an intense two-day indoctrination about how to be an army officer and what he would need to do to pass as an IG officer in the field. He was a quick learner and soon was on his way to see the President of the United States, James Buchanan, who wanted to brief him.

President Buchanan stood with his back to the room when Canyon was escorted into his private study. This was not the president's ceremonial office. This was the desk where he got his work done. Buchanan looked out at a small rose garden watching a workman cutting off the old blooms and dropping them in a refuse barrel.

"Getting to feel that way myself sometimes," President Buchanan said, turning. "Like the last rose of summer: wilting and about ready for somebody to snip me off and drop me in the barrel."

Canyon had been with the president enough by now to know some of his moods. The secret agent was as relaxed today as he always was with the president, and now he chuckled softly.

"Mister President, you don't have to worry about the barrel for a long time," Canyon said. "Your leaves are still green and your thorns are sharp, as some members of Congress have been saying recently."

President Buchanan turned, his shock of white hair unruly this morning, his sharp features now smiling.

"Canyon, you're good for me. I should keep you around here, but you have a job to do. I have an old soldier friend who I'm afraid is in trouble in Texas. I've had some disturbing reports about his performance. He's been solid as a rock for me, and I want you to go down to Fort Johnson in western Texas and see what's going on.

"We've had reports that the Comanche down there are getting rifles from somebody. Not a lot of civilians in that part of Texas yet, so there's always the chance we have a couple of rotten apples in the army who are supplying them. It might also be the Comancheros. We don't know."

Buchanan looked up at Canyon. "How do you like the uniform?"

"It's . . . a bit different, Mister President. I'm not used to the saluting, but that will come. I was never cut out to be in the army. But if I must be for a while, this seems like a fine way to start."

"Starting at the top, eh?" The president chuckled and looked back at the roses. "Any questions, Canyon?"

"Yes, sir. I have my legal powers of arrest and investigation as a special agent, but what about these eagles on my shoulders? Can I order army men around?"

"We've given you a special brevet rank of full colonel. You have all legal and military rights as any other soldier. And you are bound by all military law and procedures as any other soldier."

"Right, I'll be firm but careful."

The president returned to his big cherry wood desk and sat in the high leather chair behind it. "Canyon, Colonel Colton is a good friend. I've known him for twenty years. I've heard he's leading his troops against Comanche camps and on raiding parties. He's not supposed to be out there in the field. He's fifty-four years

11

old and should be a desk soldier now. He's pushing too hard. He wants to get good reports for his personnel file so he can get his star. I'd rather keep him a colonel than have him cut to pieces by the Comanches.''

The president sighed and seemed to change gears. ''Canyon, when you get back I have a fishing trip planned. Want to see if you've lost your touch with the trout flies.''

Canyon nodded. ''My pleasure to find out as well, Mister President.''

President Buchanan stood. He looked tired, much older than his sixty-nine years.

''Canyon,'' the president said, walking to the door. ''Jim Colton is an old soldier. Somehow I get the idea he thinks he has to sing his last soldier's song with his saber out charging to his death amid three hundred screaming Comanches. Make him understand he doesn't have to do that. He doesn't have to die to impress me. There's a place for him back here. I've cleared a spot on my advisory staff and I'm sending orders with you to bring him back here. But don't show them to him right away. I have given you a letter for him as well.

''First I want you to evaluate him and the situation and find out what's rotten down there. When it's over, bring him back with you. We'll work on a replacement for the Fourth and for Fort Johnson's commander.''

''Yes, sir,'' Canyon said, and he had walked out of the president's private office.

That had been nearly two weeks ago. Now he was here in Texas, waiting for an attack to start on the Comanches. He moved his big palomino toward the colonel. At first the regimental commander had objected to the bronze stallion being in the paddock with the army horses. But he admired the animal and realized that golden horse with the white mane and tail would be leaving soon enough with Canyon.

Colonel Colton looked at Canyon and nodded. "We're ready to move. I sent one company on a four-mile ride wide and downwind around to the left behind that hill to get downriver on them. When F Company is in position, we'll begin the attack."

Canyon watched as the remaining cavalry company moved silently through the woods and brush along the stream until their scouts stopped them. They were within two hundred yards of the enemy.

"They don't know we're here yet," the lead scout reaffirmed.

Dog Company, well below authorized strength of 101 men, now formed a line through the trees. They were three yards apart, with their rifles up and ready. The line stretched sixty troopers strong across the brush.

Canyon and Colonel Colton were in the center of the line.

"I told Captain Lancer to begin his attack as soon as he could get F Company in position. When we hear their shots, we move in."

They waited another five minutes, then a volley of rifle shots blasted into the silence of the Texas afternoon.

The bugler sounded charge when Colonel Colton pointed at him, and the sixty troopers and officers of Dog Company galloped forward through the brush and into a small valley with the Indian encampment spread out along the Brazos eighty yards ahead.

A Comanche warrior dashed from his tepee, grabbed his war lance from just outside, lifted the metal point, and impaled a cavalry private as he rode by. The point of the ten-foot shaft pierced all the way through the trooper's body, jolting him off his horse.

The man just behind the dead soldier put a .44 round

through the Comanche's chest. He had used his lance for the last time.

Women and children scattered into the brush. Two mounted troopers fighting hand to hand with one Comanche who had gained his horse raced through the side of the camp. In the struggle they did not watch where they were going. A Comanche woman carrying a baby looked up too late as the three horses swept toward her and she went down under the slashing hooves. A few seconds later the mother sprawled in the dirt and the baby lay in her dead arms, screeching in terror.

Colonel O'Grady saw four troopers fighting six mounted warriors to the right. He charged that way, firing his Spencer twice and knocking down one of the hostiles. Then he was in the middle of it.

The four troopers looked up and met another rush of the five warriors on their war ponies. The volley of rounds pushed the Comanche back. Most of the troopers had dry revolvers and had no time to reload. They swung up their Spencers and charged ahead.

Canyon fired his big army Colt .44 with ivory grips, knocking down another attacker. But the four troopers and Canyon were being pushed back, separated from the other blue-shirts.

"One man in the rear and reload," Canyon bellowed. It worked for the first man, then four more Comanches ran at them unmounted. O'Grady pulled the men back to the edge of the river and all reloaded. They were trapped against steep, precipitous banks. No way to retreat, but their backs were safe. They had to fight. The men pushed new tubes of rounds into their Spencer carbines and watched the brush near them.

"Get ready," Canyon called to the four troopers. He had seen one take an arrow in the arm and one had been shot in the thigh, but all were still fighting. "They won't leave us here long."

Just then twelve Comanches rushed at them, four of them on war ponies. The fighting sounds of the rest of the troopers showed that they had fought their way fifty yards forward, leaving Canyon and his men cut off and in trouble.

"We're on our own," O'Grady bellowed. "Make every round hit. Hold your fire until we can't miss."

Then it was past time to talk. The twelve Comanches bellowed in hatred and swarmed toward them. . . .

2

Canyon O'Grady sat steady on Cormac and concentrated on the first mounted charging Comanche, who was coming in riding off the side of his war pony and presented only one foot as a target. Canyon's shot caught the horse in the head and he fell, tripping another war pony.

Canyon shifted his aim and fired the Spencer carbine again, sending out the .52-caliber chunk of lead at a running Comanche who darted and dodged as he raced forward. Canyon's second shot burrowed through the red man's chest.

The troopers poured out a surprising amount of fire with the Spencer rifles. The Comanches, unused to the rapid-fire repeating weapons, stared in surprise; then, forty yards from their easy prey, they turned and ran into the thick brush.

The troopers had by then used up their tubes of seven rounds and were reloading. When they finished the quick process of sliding out the old tube and pushing in the new one, Canyon shouted to them. "Regroup and return to the main force!"

They followed him north toward the sound of a few shots. No more Comanche attacked. The blue-coats were in charge of the whole area. A few troopers chased running warriors into the brush and upstream.

More of the troops were in the process of pulling down the Indian tepees. Canyon was impressed by the sturdy construction of the tall shelters, yet saw how easily they could be taken down. The Indians would then use the long poles for travois and fold the big and heavy buffalo-skin tepee covers into neat bundles.

But not this time.

"Burn everything that will catch fire," Colonel Colton shouted. "Destroy all of that jerky and the pemmican. If the heathens can't eat, they won't be raiding so much."

Colton sat on his black army mount looking like he had a saber down his spine. His brown eyes showed contempt and disdain for the Comanche. His uniform was in perfect condition, if a bit dusty now from the thirty-mile ride. Every element of his manner and action indicated that he was in command.

Under his light-brown campaign hat, his hair was thick and brown, matching furious eyebrows that were so full they met between his eyes, creating one long brown hedge across his head. Hard, thin lips were now pressed together.

"Get that tepee torn down and burned, Sergeant. We can't stay here all day!" The colonel often spoke directly to the troops without going through the chain of command.

The colonel was five-ten, tall for a pony soldier, but the cavalry had been his first love during his thirty-three years in the army. He watched the destruction of the camp with a thin smile.

At the side stood an angry collection of women and children. The army had no provisions for Indian prisoners. They would be released when the camp was razed.

"If it won't burn, smash it up," Colonel Colton ordered. "We don't want to leave a stick or a pot or a buffalo robe here that the damn Comanche can use."

It took them two hours to demolish everything. When the last of the troopers came back from chasing the Comanche, they told wild tales and the sergeants had to work to get an accurate count of savages killed. They divided the troopers' numbers in half and told their lieutenants.

Captain Lancer returned with most of Company D, which had chased the Comanches who had managed to get mounted.

"We followed them almost all the way to the bluffs that lead up to the Staked Plains, but then we lost their tracks. It's a maze over there of blind canyons, false trails, and tracks."

Colonel Colton took his report and nodded. "By God, we whipped the Comanche tails today," he said. "If we could catch more of them this way, we could stop their threat in a month. Trouble is, they hear us coming or have out scouts and see us, and by the time we find a camp like this, they've packed up and moved away, leaving us forty different trails."

Canyon rode around the ruined camp. The whole place smelled like a kitchen with the burned jerky and the burning pemmican. Some of the jerky was saved for the troops. It would taste a lot better than the army ration of salt pork and hardtack.

Colonel Colton made an inspection of the area, declared the camp totally destroyed, and ordered the officers to form up the troops for a march.

He rode up to Canyon, who sat watching the men move into a column of fours by company. When the troopers surrounding the Indian women and children moved away, the Comanches screamed in anger and fury and scattered into the brush.

Colonel Colton took a casualty report from his officers. They had three dead and six wounded. All of the six could ride. The dead were draped stomach-down over their saddles, with their hands and feet tied together under the horse's belly.

It was a hot, dry, and dusty thirty-mile ride back to

Fort Johnson. The area had experienced no rain for over a month. Even the cactus looked dry. A choking cloud of dust rose from the five hundred hooves churning the sparse soil. Anyone watching could see the column coming for miles by the dust trail that rose into the stillness of the desert sky.

Not a desert, really, Canyon knew, but close enough. Maybe six to eight inches of rain a year in most of the area.

Canyon moved back to the head of Dog Company and rode beside Captain Lancer. They exchanged stories about the short, sharp battle.

"Are most of the campaigns against the Indians like this, Captain Lancer?" Canyon asked.

"No, sir. Most of them we ride a day and a half and find that the hostiles have seen us coming and vanished into the countryside somewhere. They like to run up to the Staked Plains."

"You've been in a fight or two, I'd guess, Captain?"

"Yes, sir, Colonel O'Grady. I've had ten years of fighting the Indians. It's been damn near my whole career."

"Captain, you know the normal duties of an IG."

"Yes, sir."

"I need to talk to you. Can you spare an hour or so?"

Captain Lancer grinned and Canyon liked him at once. He was burned brown by wind and sun. He rode the black mare like he was part of the animal. As with most of the cavalrymen, he was not large, maybe five-seven and slender. Exactly right to fit on a horse. He had dark hair and a crooked grin and thin blue eyes that squinted into the sun, leaving wrinkles around his eyes.

"Might have a minute, Colonel, if I can squeeze it into my loaded social calendar."

Both men laughed.

"You know I'm here concerning the good of the service. I'm not worried about individuals or personalities, except where they affect the overall performance of a unit or a fort."

The captain looked over and nodded.

"What I'm saying is, have you noticed any problems or difficulties for Colonel Colton in the performance of his duties?"

Captain Lancer heaved a long sigh and looked the other way. When he stared back at Canyon, he shrugged. "Who's to say what's normal? Every man handles the command of troops a little differently. One gripe from all of the officers you'll hear is that the colonel isn't supposed to be out here in the field. This isn't his job, isn't his place. But I'm not about to tell him that. You know a regimental commander shouldn't go out on a search-and-find raid, even with two companies of troops."

"Yes, that has been one of the worries that I have heard about. Oh, I'm sure you understand anything we say is strictly confidential. I don't want anyone else to know what we talked about."

"Yes, sir."

"I'll even tell the men in Dog Troop the same thing when I ask questions about you." Canyon chuckled, and after a moment's hesitation, Captain Lancer joined him.

"Seriously, any other situations I should know about concerning the colonel?"

"No, sir. He doesn't drink to excess, his morals are almost puritanical, he's a married man with a grown family back East. He's a good commander. Knows his men, leads by example, never takes a tent on a march when the men don't have theirs. One of the best commanders I've ever worked under."

"Fine, thanks. Part of my total job here is to make a report on the officers and commanders, as you know.

If you have anything else I should hear about concerning the fort, I hope you'll come and see me. I'll be working out of my quarters. You know the one. I'm afraid I ranked out Captain Willoughby for his bed.''

"The change will do Willoughby good," Captain Lancer said.

"Thanks, Lancer, I'll be getting back to the front."

Captain Lancer popped a smart salute to O'Grady, who remembered to return it and then rode out of the dust on the upwind side to the front of the column and moved into line beside Colonel Colton.

Six hours later the patrol pulled into the fort and formed up on the parade ground. Colonel Colton briefly thanked the men for a job well done and asked the officers to dismiss the men.

It was just after dark when Canyon O'Grady finished a relaxing bath and shaved and put on his second uniform and reported to Captain Lancer's house for supper. The invitation had been offered earlier in the day.

Lancer met Canyon at the door and waved him inside.

"My humble quarters, Colonel. Glad that you could come. My Millie is the best cook on the post and I like to show off her good cooking whenever I can."

Millie came out from the kitchen wiping her hands on a large apron. She was slender and dark with darting eyes and an infectious grin that won over Canyon at once.

"Ray, you stop with the blarney, a person would think you were Irish like the good colonel here." She held out a small hand and shook Canyon's big paw like she meant it. "I'm most pleased to meet you, Colonel O'Grady. I see a bit of the Emerald Isle in your grin and in your eyes." She smiled. "Of course the red hair isn't a giveaway at all."

"Mrs. Lancer, a pleasure to meet you. I've heard

you're a long-suffering woman to put up with the likes of the captain here.''

''The truth is finally coming out.''

They all three laughed. As they talked, a girl, about twenty years old, came from the far door. She was dark like Millie Lancer with black bangs straight across her forehead and a black raging torrent of hair down her back. She walked forward with a confident air and smiled directly at Canyon. She had the soft gray eyes that didn't miss a thing, an oval face with high cheekbones, and a small nose over a rosebud mouth that Canyon swore was so red it must have a touch of lipstick. She was slender and well-formed, with a graceful step.

''I'm the other long-suffering woman in the household,'' she said. ''I'm Lucinda, but everyone calls me Cindy.'' She reached out her hand and the Lancers smiled. He took her hand and held it a moment. It was cool and firm.

''Miss Cindy, what a pretty name. But I like Lucinda, too. More strength, more depth, more personality,'' Canyon offered.

''Now you've done it, Colonel,'' Captain Lancer said. ''We won't be able to live with our daughter for another week.''

They all laughed and went into the small living room. The quarters here were not designed for women, but did have a kitchen and two bedrooms. It was a captain's quarters, almost the same as Canyon's.

''You're from Washington, D.C.?'' Cindy asked as they all sat on the sofa and two upholstered chairs.

''Afraid so. But it isn't all that glamorous. I don't go to dinner with the president or anything like that.''

''But you have seen President Buchanan, I bet,'' Cindy said.

''Yes, I've seen him. He's a good dancer at those balls he has.''

"You've actually been to a presidential ball?" Cindy asked, her face alive with wonder and awe.

"Well, yes, but it wasn't all that exciting, and I had to leave early."

"What kind of gowns did the women wear?" Cindy asked, her eyes bright with wonder.

"Long ones," Canyon said.

"And cut low in front?" Cindy asked.

"Lucinda, what a thing to ask," Captain Lancer said sharply.

"No, not at all," Millie said. "I bet they were cut extremely low in front." Her mother grinned at her and the two went off to the kitchen to finish supper.

The two men lit long cigars and puffed a moment. Then Captain Lancer looked over at Canyon.

"Colonel, is there any way that you can convince Colonel Colton that he shouldn't be in the field so much? Some of us are very concerned. He could have picked up a stray bullet or an arrow today as well as those men we brought home belly-down over their saddles."

"You're right, Lancer. I know it and he knows it. But he's pushing for some good field experience to go on his record. The colonel has been a garrison soldier most of his career. Now he needs this Indian combat to get his first star. At least that's what he's indicated to me. He wants in my report that he takes to the field with his troops for important engagements."

"Fact is, he shouldn't be out there at all," Captain Lancer said.

"Why? Do you know something about him you're not telling me?"

"I meant tactically. A full colonel shouldn't go on patrols, much too risky."

Canyon frowned. It seemed like the captain was on the verge of telling him something more about the colonel, something that happened or some condition. Something not quite right. But the moment had passed.

"Dinner is served," Cindy said in her most formal butler's voice. Then she broke up laughing. "They call it dinner in the fancy houses in New York and even in Chicago. But out here I guess it's still supper."

Canyon seated Cindy, then went around the table and sat across from her at the neat, made-for-four table.

The dinner wasn't fancy, but wholesome and filling. Roast beef, from a dwindling herd of cattle that the fort kept after capturing them from an Indian band nearly six months ago. They had considered letting them breed and calf and have a continuing supply, but the temptation was too great, and one by one the wild-eyed Texas longhorns were dropping to the butcher's knife.

"Tell us more about Washington, D.C.," Cindy said before the fruit salad was barely begun.

"Child, the colonel has other things on his mind," Captain Lancer said.

Canyon told them about the streets and avenues all paved with cobblestones and a few even of concrete. He talked about the beautiful plantings of trees and flowers and shrubs making it like a park.

"Lots of fancy carriages and beautifully dressed men and women?" Cindy asked, her eyes wide.

Canyon laughed softly. "I think you'd like to see our nation's capital, Cindy. Perhaps your father will be stationed there sometime."

After the meal the women cleared the dishes and the men went to the living room for the rest of their pinched-out cigars.

"Colonel, I must tell you again that I'm afraid for Colonel Colton. I just have a gut feeling that he shouldn't be going on these patrols, especially when he takes command."

24

"You surely can't imagine him riding along and not being in command."

"No, sir. That's partly what troubles me. As you said, he's been a garrison soldier most of his life."

Before they could pursue that line, Cindy came back in.

"Now it's time to learn to play bridge," Cindy said, taking command of the situation. "That's the new game that all of the wives are learning. It's supposed to be quite the social thing to do these days."

They worked at it for two hours. Millie had a rule book and they kept trying.

At last Captain Lancer threw down his cards. "There are too many rules and I don't understand six of them," he said. "Let's try it another time."

Canyon felt the tension of the day recapturing him. He hadn't ever been in an army battle before. He was still stunned by it. He thanked the host, complemented Millie on her dinner, and headed for the front door.

Cindy saw him out and stepped just past the front door with him. In the darkness, she reached up and kissed his lips in a quick calculated move that surprised him.

"Handsome Canyon O'Grady, I'd love to see you again. You be sure and come back." She smiled impishly at him, whirled away, and slipped back inside the house.

Canyon stood there with a silly grin on his face, remembering the sweetness of her lips and the touch of her breasts against his chest when she kissed him. "Yes, Cindy Lancer, I will be sure to see you again," he said, and walked toward his quarters.

He had just passed the last officer's house before his own when a shadow moved in the blackness only six feet away.

"Colonel, sir?" a soft, southern voice asked.

"Yes, I'm Colonel O'Grady. What do you want?"

25

"A minute of your time, sir. I . . . I ain't used to talking to officers, sir."

"Forget I'm an officer. Talk man to man. You don't even have to show yourself. What's bothering you?"

"Sir, I don't know how to say this. I take a nip now and then. After payday last Friday I got me a little . . . drunk, you know? I passed out in the stables where I hid the bottle. Other guys drink it all up if I take it to the barracks.

"Anyway, sir, I woke up and it was dark and I heard these two men talking. I listened. They didn't know I was there. Nobody else around. Then I saw these two gents were officers, but I couldn't make out which ones.

"But I remember what they said. They were trying to figure out how to kill Colonel Colton, they was. Said the whole fort would be better off if he got shot on one of the patrols he always insisted on leading. Didn't know who to tell. Figured an IG would be right. Happened about a week ago."

There was a moment of silence.

"You hear me, Colonel? A couple of officers are planning on killing Colonel Colton!"

3

"Yes, trooper, I hear you," Canyon O'Grady said. "I understand. Thank you. Proper precautions will be taken. Did the men say anything else? Such as when they might try to kill Colonel Colton or where?"

"They talked about a patrol or an Indian fight. That would be the best time, they decided."

"But no specific day, no date?"

"No, just on a patrol."

"Thank you, trooper, you're excused now. Don't tell anyone else about this or that you talked to me. Do you understand?"

"Yes, sir."

"Trooper, thanks again."

But the soldier had already vanished into the night behind the building. Well, now . . . He had heard of such actions, happened in every army, he imagined, to junior officers and sergeants at least. But a commanding colonel?

He walked the rest of the way to his quarters, disturbed by the voice in the night. It certainly was possible. A junior officer with some real or imagined slight or insult or whose career the colonel had damaged. Possible.

It was the sort of threat for which there was only one sure solution: keep the colonel off any more engagements with the hostiles. But that solution would be nearly impossible without breaking the colonel's leg.

As Canyon lay in his bed that night, he tried to remember how many officers there were on post. In the Fourth Cavalry there should be forty-four officers. He recalled that from the material he had read about a standard cavalry regiment. But his survey of the regimental roster had shown only twenty-four officers.

Every unit in the army was far under strength. Canyon knew that a cavalry company should have three officers: a captain, a first lieutenant, and a second lieutenant. Most of the twelve companies in the regiment had only one officer, some of them two.

On the Table of Organization and Equipment, which the army called T O & E, a headquarters staff of a regiment should have nine officers: one full colonel, one lieutenant colonel, three majors, three lieutenants, and a commissioned surgeon.

But here Canyon found out there was no light colonel, only two majors and two lieutenants and a surgeon who was a captain. The officers simply had to double up on the jobs that had to be done. O'Grady had noticed that the quartermaster first lieutenant also did the duty of the regimental commissary lieutenant.

At least he had fewer officers to worry about who might be trying to shoot the colonel.

Canyon went to sleep trying to remember as many of the officers as he could whom he had met in the last two days he had been on the post.

Morning came and he heard the sergeant who had been assigned as his orderly rustling around in the kitchen. By the time Canyon was up, shaved, and dressed, Sergeant O'Hallohan had breakfast ready for him.

After the meal, Canyon went directly to Regimental Headquarters and began talking with each of the officers. He wanted to know as much about the seven other men there, besides the colonel, as he could. That used up the morning, and he went by invitation to Colonel Colton's quarters for lunch.

Mrs. Colton proved to be an ample woman, two inches shorter than her husband and about as sturdy. She had her gray hair pulled into a severe bun at the back of her head, and her whole attitude was no-nonsense.

She stared at Canyon for a moment from cold green eyes, then a hint of a smile touched her face. "Yes, the IG from Washington. Welcome to our quarters, Colonel O'Grady. We don't eat dinner here like the farmers do. Figure we should be one step removed from that heavy work, so we have a light luncheon and then our full dinner in the evening."

"Yes, ma'am," Canyon said. He held his campaign hat in his hands like a buck private, and Colonel Colton grinned.

"Jenny you don't have to be so hard on the young man. He's just here doing his job the way we're doing ours. As for me, I'm starved."

They went into the kitchen where a table was set with three kinds of sandwiches, milk, tea and coffee, and three kinds of fruit for desert.

"I'm glad you didn't go to any trouble, Mrs. Colton," Canyon said with a twinkle in his eye.

The woman only stared at him in barely concealed antagonism.

"My wife is not one to waste humor on," Colonel Colton said. He sat down and took one of each of the three kinds of sandwiches. The crust had been carefully trimmed off the fresh home-baked bread.

"Fact is my wife's sense of humor went down with the *Mayflower* in the Caribbean several years ago."

His wife looked at the colonel with little change of

expression, took a sandwich and a cup of tea, and retreated to her bedroom.

"Strategic withdrawal," Colonel Colton said. "Ever since you came here, she's been of a mind that you've come to sack me for sure. You see, O'Grady, I've been on this post for two years now, and the IG comes every eight months. We had an IG man through here three months ago. No reason you should be here—excepting that President James Buchanan himself sent you. He knows that I need some good Indian-fighting reports in my file so I can get a star pinned on my shoulder boards."

It was the longest speech Canyon had heard the colonel make since he had arrived. Canyon took a bite from one of the sandwiches. It had been filled with thinly sliced roast beef and cheese and lettuce and mustard, and was delicious.

"Colonel, you know I can't reveal my orders to you, not with my IG credentials. So why don't we forget the speculation and just let me do my job."

"Are you here to sack me, O'Grady?"

"No. Now just relax. But I can tell you that the president is concerned with your safety. He isn't exactly enthusiastic about your leading all of these patrols and engagements with the Comanche. That's a good way for a man, even a colonel, to get himself killed."

"If the president wants me to stop going into the field, he can send me a letter ordering me to stop," Colonel Colton said. "Or he can have the Department of Texas commander so order me. Without one of the two, I'm going to go right on getting into the field when I think I should."

Canyon looked up, chewed another bite, and nodded. "Damn good sandwiches, Colonel. Thank your wife for me."

They talked of other things then. The colonel was

interested in the Washington scene and who the president had as his current military advisers.

The rest of the afternoon Colonel Canyon O'Grady talked with the remaining members of the headquarters staff. He found no good prospects for the conspirators who had spoken about killing the colonel.

When he had finished talking to the last man, he took his notes back to his quarters, where a small desk had been set up with a kerosene lamp. Canyon went over his evaluations carefully.

Major Harlow Stanton: 42, overweight in rank. Short and jolly. A fat man who carried it well. Excellent horseman. A politician, gets along well with everyone. No malice in his soul. Not a suspect.

Major Winfred Westcott: 35, tall and thin. The nervous type who seems to be worried about something constantly. Friendly and helpful. Knows all the other officers. Is second in command of the fort. Seemed pleased with his position. I could find no animosity toward Colonel Colton. Westcott was a career man, had joined the army to fight in the Mexican War but saw little action there as a new second lieutenant. He went into the cavalry and served as a company commander. He had been a major for two years.

First Lieutenant Tucker Vallis: 24, adjutant. Works with me in my duties as IG. Blond, medium build. Good detail man, fine memory. Blue eyes, clean shaven. French descent. A team player. No sign of discontent with colonel, with whom he works closely.

Second Lieutenant Felix Fay: 23, quartermaster and commissary officer. Busy. A million details. Harried, nervous, but not irritable. Often with a big smile. Has never been on a patrol. Takes death of men to heart. Good officer. No apparent trouble with the colonel.

Canyon hadn't had a chance to talk to the doctor yet, but he would be in no position to have any big problems with the commander. He was still working over the wounded from the engagement the day before. Others said he was a hardworking hard-drinking medic, who had saved a lot of lives and usually went along on patrols and actions when more than a company of men were in the field.

Canyon walked to the window and stared out across the bleak, hard, and beaten-down parade grounds centered between the buildings. The fort had been built around the parade ground, which was roughly four hundred yards square. It was used for drills and parades. He could see the enlisted men's barracks on the far side, the flagpole, and to the far right, the stables, tack rooms, and paddock area.

Just another army fort. But one where two officers were planning on killing the commander. All Canyon had to do was find out which two out of the twenty-four officers on the base. There were about seven hundred and eighty soldiers stationed here. What if that trooper had been mistaken and the plotters were really enlisted men? Then the odds of finding the conspirators would be tremendously higher.

O'Grady turned for the door and took a long walk around the fort thinking through his interviews. No one stood out as a possible culprit. He'd have to go through the twelve company officers. Only two of them had more than one officer. That seemed dangerously low. He remembered hearing that on a patrol like the one he went on, they had to borrow officers from other troops to put two officers with each company in the field.

On his way back from his walk, Canyon went past Captain Lancer's quarters. Cindy was in the doorway shaking out a dusting cloth. She smiled and waved, but he went on past. A diversion would be nice about now. Let his mind work over the data he had supplied it today.

But it would be too big a risk, a diversion with

Cindy. Her father might demand satisfaction on the end of a pair of pistols. Even though dueling was outlawed in the army and in the nation, more than a thousand duels were still fought each year, he had been told.

Canyon shrugged, went back to his quarters to see what his orderly had prepared for supper. There was an officers' dance and reception in his honor that evening. He wasn't sure who had arranged it, but all of the officers and their wives and danceable daughters would be there.

Canyon hoped that it would be more interesting than the bridge game he had had to endure last night. As he thought of it, he figured this would be one more way to get a look at the officers he hadn't seen yet, to evaluate them. The killers could just as well come from the companies as from headquarters.

He arrived a little late, after the dancing had started. That way he was sure to find the right quarters. The affair was at Major Stanton's. The living-room furniture had been carried out on the porch, except for a few chairs, and the dining-room things had been pushed back to the walls to make a respectable dance floor.

The major's quarters had the only piano on the post. It was taken around here and there where it was needed. Tonight it formed the foundation for the orchestra. Two fiddlers, a banjo player, and a guitarist made up the group. They were all enlisted men and were getting paid three dollars each for the session. That was a third of a month's pay, so they played whenever called.

Canyon O'Grady made sure his uniform was precisely correct, then he marched up the steps and into the living room.

A short blond lady with an overflowing bosom came rushing up, smiling and nodding.

"You must be Colonel O'Grady. Welcome to the ball. I'm Mrs. Stanton, and I hope you have a wonderful time. Welcome to the post, welcome to Texas. The punch bowl is right over there and I do believe one of the naughty men has slipped something stronger than water into it."

She beamed at him, led him to the punch bowl, and handed him a cup, then turned to some more hostess duties.

Captain Lancer came out of the crush of bodies and said hello. "Well, Colonel, glad you could make it. We don't have one of these blowouts very often and your arrival was the best excuse we've had for months."

The music was stomping and twanging and Mrs. Stanton surged up and held out her arms.

"First dance goes to the hostess," she said, and O'Grady swept her onto the floor in a stately waltz. As they danced, he watched the others. There were twenty-four officers there, or would be shortly. On a post like this a dance was never bypassed. It was a time to see and be seen by the other officers and to try to impress them.

Women were in short supply. He had heard that only ten of the officers at the fort were married. Those wives, with maybe two or three daughters, would have to suffice for partners. He saw Cindy Lancer about then and she winked at him as she danced with some tall, rawboned second lieutenant who was talking fast and watching her like he wanted to take a bite out of her neck.

"So, how do you like our little fort here in Texas so far, Colonel O'Grady?" Mrs. Stanton asked.

"I really haven't seen much of it yet, but I will. Part of my job. You're army, you know that."

"About your job. The regular IG was here three months ago, so the tongues are wagging. Curious, you know. We know it isn't just a routine IG visit, but nobody can figure out why you're here."

"Let's hope it stays that way, Mrs. Stanton. That will make my job that much easier."

She looked at him sharply and he laughed, then she laughed and the dance was over. He thanked her and walked quickly toward Cindy, who was talking with the tall shavetail.

"The next dance, Miss Lancer?" Canyon asked when he reached her side.

The young second lieutenant turned, anger starting on his face. It vanished in a moment when he saw the silver eagles on Canyon's shoulder boards.

"Of course, Colonel O'Grady." She nodded at the tall boy and he gave a curt start of a bow and backed away.

Cindy looked up at Canyon as they waited for the music to start. Her bangs were freshly trimmed, her black hair had been brushed twenty thousand times until it glistened and hung down her back to her waist with only a few waves in the fall. Her smile was radiant.

"Oh, Lord, but I'm glad you came. That was four dances with Vincent, and to tell you the truth, I can't stand him. But where there are so few unmarried men, a dance is a dance."

"Out of fourteen you haven't found a suitable one yet?" Canyon asked with a grin.

"Don't be ridiculous! Of the fourteen only two are anywhere near passable. I'd bet that everyone of the fourteen never gets beyond captain before retirement. That includes the two who are already captains."

"You make quick evaluations."

"Not quick, I've been here for two years now. Mama is willing to do almost anything to get us back into civilization. She would take Omaha, but she would prefer Chicago. We spent four years there just before coming here.''

The music had started and they moved out in a lively two-step.

"My, you are a good dancer," she said.

"Only when I have an outstanding partner," Canyon said, and she grinned.

"See, that's what I mean. None of the other men on this post would think of saying that, of complimenting a lady. They expect me to do all the talking, and be bright and witty."

They danced through the three short numbers, applauded, and danced the next waltz. On one dance she turned the wrong way and fell against him, her breasts pressing hard against his chest.

"Oh, sorry," she said. She lowered her voice to a whisper. "But it did feel delightful there for a moment."

A minute later Major Stanton cut in and Canyon moved to the punch bowl. If there had been any whiskey or gin added to the mixture, it was a small amount. He began talking with a Captain Quinlin, and a Captain Tabler came up and introduced himself as the sawbones.

"Finally patched up those six you men got shot up a couple of days ago, or was it yesterday? I lose track of time. They all should be fine."

"Doctor, I understand you had an emergency while we were out on patrol."

"Indeed I did. That's why I couldn't go with you. Delivered a seven-and-a-half-pound baby boy. Came right on the day he was supposed to. But he's a third child, so that's not unusual." The doctor filled his punch cup and drifted away.

The rest of the evening Canyon danced with ten of the thirteen females at the affair. He talked with a dozen officers and knew he wouldn't remember their names. Nothing seemed out of place. He saw no small cliques discussing rebellion or mutiny.

The clock turned around to nearly midnight and he saw one or two of the women staring at him. Then he remembered. He was the guest of honor, and no one could leave before he did. He found his hat and saber and thanked the hostess and the major, then slipped out the front door and walked back to his quarters about fifty yards down officers' row.

He took his time. It was a pleasant fall evening. The air still not chill, and a billion stars smiling down at him. He found the Big Dipper and followed the outside stars of the cup along a straight line to the North Star.

The Dipper was to the left of the star, its handle nearly straight up and the two pointer stars coming from about the eight-o'clock position. That made it midnight by startime.

He looked at the stars a minute more, then opened his door and went inside. The pale light of a kerosene lamp showed from his bedroom. His orderly must have left it on for his convenience. He walked to the door and pushed it open.

Cindy Lancer sat on his bed. As he came in the doorway, she dropped the top of her dress.

"Hi, Canyon. I've been waiting for you."

4

Canyon O'Grady sucked in a breath. She was intoxicating; her strong smooth shoulders with breasts, generously formed, swayed and jiggled now from her movement and started a surge of hot blood into his groin. He hurried toward her.

"You shouldn't be here," he said.

"I know, but I had to come. I couldn't stand another hour without you."

He caught her shoulders, and her arms went around him; her lips touched his, then her mouth opened and their tongues tangled in a love match. Slowly he pressed her bare enticing body tightly against his chest, her breasts burning through his shirt, making his blood boil and his breath come quicker.

Canyon let her go and stepped back, to stare at her. Perfect large breasts, with cherry-red nipples already growing and pulsating with her desire.

"God, I've wanted to kiss you that way ever since the first day I saw you ride in." The pink circles around her breasts glowed and she stepped off the bed so he could see she wore nothing. He devoured her body with his glance; her swinging breasts, her small waist, the delightful swelling at the hips and down to her dark swatch of fury protection. Her legs were sleek, slender, yet muscled, and she moved now, stepping closer to him, pulling at the buttons on his uniform.

Her dark bangs moved gently as she undid fasteners and yanked off his officer's jacket, then his shirt.

"Oh, God, it makes me weak just watching you undress. Hurry!" Her hands fondled his chest and played with his chest hair, then she caught his face in her hands and pulled it down to her breasts.

He kissed her softly between her mounds, then worked lower, climbing to the peak on the right. Cindy's breath came in quick panting gasps now as his lips moved closer and closer up the slope toward her pulsating nipple.

When he kissed it, she moaned. "Oh, God, that's wonderful. So . . . marvelous . . . so great!" Then his tongue washed her hot nipple and she sagged against him, her eyes closed, her body throbbing with emotion and passion.

"I'm going to die. Damn, but that feels wonderful. How could I have waited so long for your kisses?"

Gently she pulled him to the bed, his mouth still on her breast. She lifted his lips from her mound and met them with hers. She panted and her mouth opened as they fell on the bed and rolled over until he was halfway on top of her.

She helped him strip away the rest of his clothes, then pushed him down on his back and smiled as she drank in the perfect symmetric male form, naked and aroused.

"Such marvelously strong shoulders, and your chest so full and muscled. I love the red hair on your chest, so soft and fine. Such a small waist and slender hips. Your legs look like a runner's, hard, strong, powerful. Then the best part." She bent and touched his throbbing maleness. "Beautiful!" A tear slipped out of her eye and ran down her cheek.

He pulled her down on top of him, his hands caressing her hot breasts, bringing small singing sounds from her throat.

"They love your touch, they swoon at how you play them, like a fine organ."

Canyon's hand worked lower as her passion built. It trailed down her flat belly to the surprising stiffness of her black forest. Cindy gasped as his hand pushed over her small mound.

"Oh, Lord! So fine . . . so damned fine!" Her voice rose in a wail of pleasure and desire. "Touch me there, touch me," she demanded in a wild shriek.

His hand slid around her soft, moist heartland, down her sleek inner thigh, and she crooned at him. "Yes, yes, yes! Dear Canyon, that . . . is . . . so . . . fine!" Her hand reached between them and found his hardness and held it as if it were a lifeline.

Canyon's hand drifted upward on her delicate, sensitive inner thigh almost to her damp place, slid around it, and then her hand caught his and pushed it over her treasure.

"Touch me there, right there, damn you."

His hand pressed at the moist spot, his fingers stroking the tender flesh, her wet outer lips swollen and throbbing.

Cindy gasped, then trilled as he caressed her damp center. "Oh, Lord . . . yes, yes." A moment later he hit the small node and her whole body began to quiver and then to shake, and her sudden shout of joy shattered into a thousand gasps of pleasure as tremors rattled through her a hundred times.

Cindy gasped for breath when her body quieted, sucking in enough to replace the surge of the drain on her body. Then her hips ground against his hand and one of her legs stretched across his thigh and she pushed hard, then she sat up. She kissed his lips, then both his eyes, and moved down his chest, spreading hot, furious kisses as she went.

"You taste delicious, the best man meat in the world." Cindy sang a little song as she kissed down his chest through his mat of red hair, across his slightly curved belly and to the start of his red tangle of fur.

Cindy leapt it, caught his stiff maleness in one hand, and kissed the heavy member a dozen times. "Oh, my! Wonderful."

"Good, Cindy. Yes," Canyon shouted, and then moaned in delight. He felt his desire surging, but he beat it back and found her sleek body with his hands, reaching for one of her hanging breasts.

Cindy fell away from him on her back. "Oh, God, right now!" She caught at him, pulled him toward her, then on top of her. She spread her legs and lifted her feet high in the air. "Right now before I die," she shouted. "Quick, O'Grady." Cindy panted as she caught his shoulders, then his hips, and slammed him downward and toward her.

Canyon watched her a moment, then eased between her soft tender white thighs.

She helped, pulling him, positioning him. "Oh, God I can't wait. I'm going to explode. I know I will." She pulled him forward, pushing up with her hips, and then squealed in total erotic pleasure as he slid into her and she pounded upward to capture all of him. "Yes . . . yes . . . Oh, damn that's good. More, O'Grady, more." She humped her hips as high as she could, then a long low wail of joy, acceptance, and victory gushed from her throat. The primal wail of total pleasure roared for a moment, then trailed off into a contented sigh.

Her hips began to grind against him and she bounced upward with his every thrust.

Now Cindy panted in rhythm, and her hips lifted.

"Oh, God . . . so good . . . fantastic . . . never better!"

Then she erupted again; her wail reached a shriek and her whole body quivered, trembled, and a dozen times she shook as if an earthquake rattled her. Her

41

hips pounded upward and she wailed and moaned, her hips thrusting up as high as she could reach. She held the position for one long delicious extra moment of desire fulfilled, then she collapsed and he went with her to the softly rocking motion of the bed.

Canyon realized that he had spilled over the top of his own limit sometime during her last rush, and he was drained and spent. Now he eased down on top of her.

"So delicious, so good, Canyon O'Grady. So good." She reached around his back and gripped her hands together. "Now I'll never let you go. I have to recover before I can even sit up."

They lay there for ten minutes, then she stirred and he rolled away from her. She cuddled against him not wanting it to end.

"How did you get out of your father's house?" Canyon asked.

"I have a large window in my bedroom. I left the dance early with my mother and went to bed with a pounding headache. I always lock my door inside." She pressed against him, her bare breasts tightly against his chest. "This is so good. I want to stay here all night."

"That will get me shot in the morning."

"The army doesn't shoot colonels that easily."

"I hope not." He eased upward and she held him a moment, then let go. They both sat up. He bent and kissed her still-hot breast. "Damn good," he said.

"We'll have to try it again, just to see if it can be so good again."

"It will be. I'll help you dress."

She let him, then they kissed again, their mouths open, tasting each other, almost falling over on the bed once more. He pushed away.

"Yes, we'll try again sometime later. You hurry right home."

"Yes, sir," she said, and gave him a mock salute. He eased open the front door and looked out. He saw no one. She kissed him, slipped out the door, and walked quietly around to the back of his quarters and down to her father's.

Canyon closed the door, barred it, and slid back into bed. He thought for a moment about how it would be, being married and not having to sneak around for sex. Sure, marriage had its advantages, but a lot of the other kind as well. Marriage wasn't for Canyon O'Grady, not for a few good years yet. He turned over and went to sleep.

The next morning, after breakfast, O'Grady had a quiet talk with the Fort Johnson commander. Canyon didn't think it was the right time to tell the commander about the death threat by the two officers. He wanted to impress on the colonel that this trip was not a try to get his job or downgrade him in any way.

Colonel Colton stared up at Canyon as soon as he came into the room.

"We need to have a man-to-man talk, O'Grady. Don't try to pull rank on me because my date of rank is about five years before yours. Listen to me."

Canyon sat down in the chair beside the desk and waited.

"I'm doing what I want to do. I have a fort to command, I have seven hundred troops. I'm doing a fairly good job against the Comanche. This is one of the toughest posts in the army right now in 1860. Who knows what it will be like in another two or three years.

"You've probably got reports about me. Hell, O'Grady, I know how the fucking army works. I've been in it for thirty-three years. I just got a little too hot that day and my eyes went bad for a couple of minutes. Black spots, nothing to worry about.

"Look, O'Grady, unless you're blind, you know that

there is a big war coming up. Not the Indians. With the South. Already some of the Deep South states are talking secession, forming an independent country down there. Congress won't stand for that, so we'll have a war and it's gonna be a big one.

"I'm going to be part of it. Hell, we have about twenty thousand troops in the whole army right now. If we go to war against the South, we'll have conscription and volunteer regiments and maybe a million men under arms. I'll get my stars in quick order and be in the thick of it. You can't cut me out of my life's ambition.

"You hear what I'm saying, O'Grady? In two years or less this country is going to be in the biggest damn war we've ever known."

"There has been a lot of talk and speculation about that subject in Washington, Colonel Colton. Sure, I've heard it. I can't tell you what's going to happen, but if the South does decide to leave the Union, then we'll have to stop them by force of arms."

"Exactly. Now, why the hell are you here on my post from the IG's office?"

"Normal inspection tour. We're changing the scheduling to match with some other changes."

Colonel Colton threw a riding crop across the room and turned his back on Canyon for a moment. When he faced the special agent again, most of the red flush had left his face. "All right, O'Grady, stick to your story. I know you can't tell me, but I have a right to ask." Colonel Colton pounded his palm against the desk.

"Damnation! You want to find out about that patrol, you go talk to Captain Lancer. He's the best Indian fighter we have on the post and I always take him with me. He'll never volunteer to tell you anything, but you tell him I said he should explain exactly what happened, no matter how bad it looks for me. That should simplify your work here and get you out of my hair faster."

"Thanks, Colonel. I appreciate that. Oh, I have been instructed to give you this letter from the White House when I thought it was the right time. Seems like now."

Canyon handed the colonel the letter he had hand carried from President Buchanan.

Colton looked at it, saw the scrawled signature in the upper left-hand corner, and grinned. "At least the old fart hasn't forgotten me completely. He taught me how to hunt pheasants when I was growing up in Pennsylvania."

"I'll leave you to your letter, Colonel. Thanks for the suggestion about Captain Lancer."

Colonel Colton watched Canyon leave his office, then took out a penknife and carefully slit the official White House envelope and removed the letter. It also was on official stationery. It was two pages long in the president's usual open, easy-to-read hand.

> White House, Washington D.C.
> September 2, 1860

Dear James,

Yes, it's been a long time since I've written you. Maybe we can get together for some pheasant hunting before long. Hope your assignment there in Texas is what you wanted. You've been there two years now, that should be enough. If you're looking for a new post, be sure to let me know and I'll plead your case with the appropriate general.

The situation here grows worse by the day. Frankly I don't know if we can hold the Union together or not. I thought my popular sovereignty and choice by state constitutions for free or slave states would be enough. But it really doesn't look like that is the answer. We shall see. Another year or so will tell the tale, I'm afraid.

I trust your wife and family are all in good health. Give my best regards to that excellent cook, your wife. I don't see how you stay so trim with all that good food around.

I'm sending a good man to look over your operation. Nothing serious, so don't get alarmed. He's on a special mission for me and not entirely IG, but no one but you should know that. I can't tell you exactly what it is, but don't be dismayed. In any event, I have some plans for you that may surprise you.

Now I see it's time I have to talk to a delegation of senators, and it's not wise even for a president to keep those raucous solons waiting. Keep your health and don't let the Comanches take what hair you have left. As they used to say on the frontier a hundred years ago, "Keep one hand on your rifle and the other hand on your hair."

God be with you and yours, James Henry, and fight the good fight.

Sincerely, James Buchanan,
President of the United States

Colonel Colton lifted his brows in wonder. The president had vaguely alluded to two or three different things, but he had committed himself to nothing. Colton smoothed the folds in the linen paper and put the two-page letter and the envelope in a larger envelope. He would save that letter for his grandchildren. First he would show it to his wife. That should lift even her spirits.

Dammit, he would ride with the patrols and he would be in on every action against the Comanche that he could. Each engagement was written up and forwarded with three copies to the Department of Texas headquarters in San Antonio and to the Division of the Missouri general headquarters in Chicago. One report would go in his permanent history file. With enough in the file he would have a much better chance of winning his first star.

He sighed and stared out the window at the parade grounds. One of the companies was out there working on close order riding drills. That was what kept them sharp for engaging the enemy.

Colonel Colton knew he had to last another year. By that time he figured the war would be started and they would need every field grade officer they had. He would get a division at least and perhaps a three- or four-division army. Yes, that sounded so sweet. He had put in his time and paid his dues and let enough blood for the army. He was due.

Colonel Colton wished now that he hadn't told O'Grady about Captain Lancer. There could still be time. He could send for Captain Lancer and order him not to tell the IG man a thing about that raid they made on the Comanche two months ago. He hadn't had a bit of eye trouble since then. It had to be eye problems. That was all it could be. He would have his eyes checked by Tabler one of these days.

There was no rush on that.

What about Captain Lancer? Should he call him in and prevail upon him as a friend and comrade under arms not to tell O'Grady everything he knew?

The colonel watched the troops wheeling about and coming into a company front, then quickly regrouping in their workout on the parade ground.

There was little choice. He had to talk to Captain Lancer before O'Grady did. He called in his sergeant and had him send someone to find Captain Lancer and bring him into the office at once.

5

Canyon O'Grady had left Regimental Headquarters and walked directly to Dog Company's orderly room, where he talked to Captain Lancer. They went across the quadrangle to O'Grady's quarters and had the sergeant make coffee for them.

"Captain, as I told you in your office, you and I must have a confidential talk about exactly what happened to Colonel Colton when you went on that patrol with him about two months ago."

"I'm not sure which one you mean, Colonel. There have been a lot of patrols."

"I'm sure there have, but you remember this one. This was the time that the colonel had trouble with his eyes. He said he had some black spots for a moment. I want you to tell me what really happened."

Captain Lancer looked across the room without meeting Canyon's eyes.

"Captain, I know you're loyal to your colonel. That is admirable. But if there is some problem no one is talking about, there could be a chance that you and half of your men could be slaughtered by the Comanche because something went wrong at the command level. Neither of us wants that to happen, do we, Captain Lancer?"

"No, sir, certainly not. I'm not sure I can help you much. We were on a routine patrol when we happened on a dust trail that turned out to be a band of some forty Comanche warriors heading straight for us. We were at a water hole and they needed it. We guessed that they were on a raid toward southern Texas or maybe into Mexico for horses and women. That's how the Comanche live. They don't farm or raise cattle for a living; they raid anyone they can get to. Horses can be sold to the Comancheros for whatever they need.''

''So what happened to Colonel Colton?''

''I'm not sure, Colonel. He said we would attack them from the ambush we had set up along the trees near this small stream. We waited and waited, and the order never came. The hostiles kept coming closer and closer. Just before the warriors were to the trees, maybe twenty yards away, I gave the order to fire and we attacked and chased them halfway back to their camp. We didn't lose any men because of the lack of an order from the colonel.''

''But you had to give the command to fire. Why didn't Colonel Colton call out the order?''

''I asked him the same thing when I came back. He told me that he was overly hot and that some black spots kept bothering his eyes until he had to close them. It sounded reasonable to me, so I never said anything about it. Hell, I've had those black spots in my eyes. Sometimes when I raise up too fast everything goes black for a few seconds.''

''But not for two hundred yards as an Indian pony would walk. Shouldn't you have started firing at a hundred yards?''

''Yes, sir, that was to be the firing distance.''

''It would take an Indian pony two or three minutes to walk a hundred yards, wouldn't you think?''

''At least two minutes, sir.''

''So his vision was flawed for two minutes. And you didn't think this was unusual?''

''No, sir. It didn't seem so at the time. We didn't

lose a man on that engagement and sixteen Comanche warriors died on the prairie that day.''

"So it became a victory, a fine killing patrol for the glory of Colonel Colton?''

"He was in command, sir. You know the army.''

"Was the problem his eyes, or was it something else, Captain?''

"I'm not sure what you mean.''

"I've seen men freeze up in a tense situation. You've seen a man unable to move due to fear or some other emotion in an attack by Indians, haven't you?''

"Yes, sir. Just once. The man was butchered by the Comanche because he wouldn't get down into the safety of a ditch. He simply couldn't move. But nothing like that happened to the colonel, I'm sure. I saw him just before I hunkered down behind a big rock. He was perfectly calm, in control of himself.''

Canyon poured more coffee in the captain's cup. Sergeant O'Hallohan brought out a plateful of just-baked cinnamon rolls.

Captain Lancer nodded. "About time you got some here, O'Hallohan. I was wondering if you were slipping.''

"Waiting for the best time, sir,'' the big sergeant with short red hair said.

Colonel O'Grady looked at the captain.

"O'Hallohan here is the best cook in the regiment. He and three others were in a contest to see which one got to be your orderly. He won with his cinnamon rolls. Usually he's my orderly, but I'm loaning him to you.''

The cinnamon rolls were some of the best Canyon had ever tasted. Thick cinnamon-sugar syrup coated almost all of the rolled-up cake dough. Chopped walnuts on top added to the zest.

The two officers were silent a few minutes as they ate at the hot rolls and sipped the coffee.

"Captain Lancer, since that time, two months ago, how many patrols have you ridden with the colonel?"

"Average one a week. Seven or eight. Including the one you were on with us."

"Have you noticed any other instances where the colonel did not seem to be in total control of the situation?"

"No, sir. Not once. We had four engagements with the hostiles out of that number, which is remarkably high. But not once did he have eye trouble again. Oh, well, there was one time . . . But that was when we were riding back. It was hot and we had just eaten and the colonel seemed to fall asleep as we were riding. But that's no problem. I've slept for five miles at a time on occasion on the return ride."

"You know for sure he was napping, Captain?"

"Well, not for sure, but he seemed to be drifting off to sleep now and then."

They worked on the cinnamon rolls again. When they each had eaten two of the six on the tray, Canyon stood.

"Captain, I don't want you to say one word to anyone about what we've been talking about here. This is top secret, understand? This is just between the two of us. If the colonel asks you what we talked about, say about the patrol. He was the one who asked me to contact you. But don't go into any details."

"Yes, sir. I'm familiar with the IG routines."

"Good. If you think of anything else I need to know, I'd be pleased if you'd contact me so we can talk."

"I'll be glad to do that, sir. Is there anything else?"

"No, Captain, I think that's all. Except for one thing. Why don't you have one more cinnamon roll to eat on your walk?"

Captain Lancer grinned, took the roll, and marched out of O'Grady's quarters.

The rest of the day, Canyon tried to make some sense

out of the facts and impressions that he had gathered so far. At last he went to see the doctor, Captain Tabler. The man was young, not much over thirty-five. Most doctors in the military seemed to be older.

"Doc, you have any kind of an eye test you can give me?" Canyon asked after the preliminaries were over.

"You having trouble seeing?"

"Not a lot. Seems like my right eye is a little stronger than my left."

"Not unusual. I have some eye charts somewhere, but they don't tell me a lot."

"What about black spots in front of my eyes?"

"Not a big problem, as long as it happens when you straighten up quickly after bending over. They tell me that this is because your rapid movement pulls blood away from the back of your eyes and that messes up the optic nerve, or something like that. Hell, I'm no eye expert."

"What if the spots just happened, without the movement?"

"Don't know. Could be dozens of causes, I'd think. Like I say, I'm no expert on eyes. You wait until you get back to Washington and go to one of them fancy specialists. Anything else bothering you? I'm better on broken bones and gunshot wounds than anything else."

Canyon stood and waved. "When I get either one, I'll come running right over here."

"Good, the ones I don't like are the ones they have to carry in on a stretcher."

The men said good-bye and Canyon went out the door, not knowing much more about black spots in front of eyes than he did before the visit.

That same evening just after dusk, two riders left the rear door of the paddock and rode due west of the fort. There was little in that direction until you came to New Mexico. Few settlers had come this far west in Texas. The riders both carried Springfield percussion rifles, model 1855, with which half of the regiment was armed.

They rode two miles to a feeder stream and stopped near a tall cottonwood and waited.

"Bang, you're dead," a voice said from the blackness.

Both men jumped to their feet from where they had been sitting beside the stream. A man came out of the shadows leading a thin, desert-adapted black mare.

"Right on time, gents," the stranger said. He moved forward. "You bring the merchandise?"

"A sample. Did you bring money?"

"No, I brought something as good as gold." The man struck a stinker match, let it flare, and then showed them a worn leather pouch. Inside was a half cup of gold dust and small nuggets.

"Be damned," the taller of the two soldiers said. "Where in hell did you get it?"

"Comanche called it woman's clay. No good for anything, but the women like the color, so they melt it and make trinkets."

"Damned expensive trinkets. How much of it you got?"

"Enough to pay you. How many rifles can you bring?"

"Get you ten this time. We have to be careful. But you must promise not to sell them to the Comanche in this area. We don't want our own rifles killing our own troopers."

"Hell, no. I wouldn't do that to you. Take them way up into New Mexico and Colorado. Got better markets up there, anyway."

"They'll cost you three ounces of gold per rifle. That's for genuine government issue Springfield 1855 models."

"Hey, too damn much! I can get them for forty dollars anyplace I want to."

"Yeah, but you'll have a longer ride. Make you a deal. You take fifteen rifles and you can have them for fifty dollars each, two and a half ounces of gold."

The stranger laughed. "Not a bad price for a twelve-dollar rifle." He scowled in the soft moonlight, shrugged. "What the hell, you got my back to the wall. Fifty it is, in gold. That's over two pounds of gold."

"True, but we're looking at thirty years in prison if we get caught. Our risk, our profit."

"Deal." He held out his hand. "Long Jack's word is his bond. I'll have the gold here tomorrow night, and you have the rifles. Wrap them in canvas so they won't get wet if'n I run into some rain or snow. Seven in one package, and eight in another."

"These won't be new weapons, you know that, Long Jack."

"Know it, but they better be in working order. You guarantee it for fifty dollars."

"We guarantee it," the taller, thin man said. He had done all of the talking for the pair.

Long Jack took out a bottle. "Seal the deal with a drink," he said. He swigged from the bottle and passed it to the taller man, who held the bottle to his lips for a time but didn't drink. The second soldier tilted the bottle and drank and coughed and sputtered.

"What is that, turpentine?" the second man bellowed.

"Damn near. Just wondered if you could talk." Long Jack corked the bottle, turned, and vanished into the darkness.

Major Winfred Westcott looked at his shorter companion and nodded. "We just made ourselves seven hundred and fifty dollars clear profit, Lieutenant Hartsook. You realize that? Three hundred and seventy-five dollars each. That's more than your entire year's pay."

"If we can get five more rifles. I told you ten was all I could get. We have had them surveyed out as unrepairable, junk. Where the hell we getting five more?"

"Get one from each of five of the companies. Hell, steal them if you have to. Or buy five for ten dollars each. You can find five men willing to sell their weapons and claim they were lost on a patrol."

The two officers rode back toward the fort, parted a half-mile away, and came in at different points. The major's horse was put away long before the lieutenant came in. No one could tie them together.

It was Thursday night, time for the poker game Major Westcott hosted each week in his larger quarters. He was not married, but his orderly always had desserts for them to eat. They played for an hour, the desserts were served, and the orderly was excused for the night.

Then the real meeting began.

Major Westcott looked around at the other three men. Lieutenant Hartsook was there, along with Captain Erin Delaney and Captain Lewis Philburton.

They waited until the sergeant had left the quarters, then Captain Delaney brought up the point they all had been thinking of.

"Maybe there's a chance this IG colonel is here especially to get rid of our beloved Colonel Colton."

"Maybe, but it's not a good bet," Westcott said. "He didn't really ask me any leading questions about the colonel. Hell, everyone knows I'm loyal to the good colonel. We can't take that chance. I suggest we move as quickly as we can."

"Even with the IG man here at the fort?" Hartsook asked. "Isn't that inviting trouble?"

"No more than ordinarily," Captain Delaney said.

"Hell, any investigation of an 'accident,' say, would have to be done by the local command anyway."

The four officers looked at one another.

"How long we been playing poker on Thursday nights?" Major Westcott asked.

"Three months, a week shy of four months," Hartsook said.

"Sounds like a damn good alibi to me," Captain Delaney said.

"But we won't use it," the major went on. "This accident has to be in combat, under fire. It has to take place the next time one of our patrols runs into the Comanche."

"Is one of us going to do it?" Captain Philburton asked. "Which one? Sounds too damn dangerous to me."

"Not one of us—hell, no," Major Westcott said. "We hire a trooper to do the job. Shouldn't be hard. He does it; we pay him, say, two hundred dollars; and he grabs a horse as soon as he gets back to the fort and rides for Austin and is never seen or heard of again. Only the man who recruits him will know who he is, so it will cut down on the possibility of any problems."

"How do we find the man?" Lieutenant Hartsook asked.

"We already have him," Westcott said. "He's been in line and waiting for our go-ahead for a month now."

"He's got my vote," Hartsook said.

The others all agreed.

"The pot's right, now all we have to do is play out the hand," Westcott said. "Our only problem is how to get this man on every patrol that's going out. He might have to go on two or three before there's any engagement with the damn Comanche."

"We can work that out," Captain Philburton said.

"I'm the one who knows who the man is, and I'll get the job done."

Major Westcott grinned. "Gentlemen, it seems we've reached a meeting of minds. We'll be back here for poker next Thursday night unless something unforeseen happens to our regimental commander."

They lifted their coffeecups in a toast and all left, quietly returning to their quarters.

Major Westcott grinned after they had gone. One more week, just one more week and he might be much, much closer to commanding his own regiment! But he wasn't going to make any waves. Things could go wrong. They had before. Now all he could do was sit tight and hope that everyone did his job. Especially the man with the rifle who would zero in on Colonel Colton on the next Comanche firefight!

6

Friday morning about ten, a runner came with a message for Canyon O'Grady in his quarters. He was requested to come to regimental HQ to talk with the commander.

Canyon put on his shirt, made sure his uniform was in proper order, and walked the two hundred yards to the GHQ. The sergeant major showed him directly into the colonel's office.

Two men were there besides the colonel. One, an Indian with one long braid down his back, wore a blue army shirt and cut-off civilian pants and moccasins. The other was a corporal who was tired, trail-worn, and looked about ready to drop.

"Wanted you to see the new look in Indian scouting, O'Grady. This is One Hand Ready and Corporal Hoover. They're just back from a long-range scouting trip. Tell the colonel how you function, Corporal."

"Well, sir, we travel only at night so the hostiles can't spot us coming. We work into probable areas where the Comanche have summer-camped before. One Hand knows many of these locations. We move at night on horseback and sniff for camp-fire smoke. We simply ride a circuit until we find a camp. Then we come back and report it, again moving only at night so we can't be seen by the Comanche."

Colonel Colton sat there beaming. "You see, Colonel O'Grady, there are a few new wrinkles an old soldier can use. Corporal Hoover and I figured this one out. That's why we find Comanche three out of five times we go out. Most army patrols have an engagement with the hostiles one in fifteen trips.

"Just so you'll know, we'll be taking sixty men out on this patrol. The camp is about thirty miles from here so we can travel four hours in daylight and the rest of the way in the dark. We'll get in position and hit the camp at dawn. We'll be taking Baker Company with Captain Lancer as my second in command." The commander looked at Canyon for a response.

"I thought Captain Lancer was the CO of D Company," Canyon said.

"He is, but Baker has only one officer, First Lieutenant Johnson is the CO, so he needs another field officer." Colonel Colton smiled. "You are welcome to come along if you'd like, Colonel. Or isn't this field work compatible with your other duties?"

"I'll be ready. When is boots and saddles?"

"Gets dark about seven P.M., so we'll be out the front gate by three this afternoon."

"I'll be there."

"You still have that new Spencer repeater carbine?"

"I do. I'm going to sight it in before we go. Oh, a question. I haven't noticed any target practice by your troops. Is the edict prohibiting practice still on?"

"It is. Damned foolishness. Tools of the trade. What good is a carbine or a rifle if the soldier using it can't hit what he's aiming at."

"I agree completely. Is there time for an hour of target practice before we go?"

Colonel Colton grinned and jumped up. "Damned right! Sergeant Major," he bellowed.

Before noon, Canyon heard rifle fire coming from the near side of the fort. He had noticed a makeshift target range there a few days ago. Good.

Canyon had two hours of sleep, then had Sergeant

O'Hallohan awaken him. He ate a large meal before reporting with his big palomino at the parade grounds at three. He had taken time out to brush down the golden animal, give him an apple and two lumps of sugar, and then saddle him gently. Canyon wanted to do more training with Cormac so he could guide him with his knees the way the Indian warriors trained their war ponies. But this took a lot of time and he just hadn't been able to do it.

He could drop the reins and use both hands on a rifle, and keep Cormac charging straight ahead. But turning him with knee signals was still only a dream.

They rode out promptly at three P.M. One officer's wife and three enlisted wives were there to see their men go off to battle. This was an expected engagement, not just a patrol, and there was the fear in the women's eyes no matter how they tried to hide it.

The regimental and the company guidons flapped in a light Texas breeze as they headed thirty miles out the Brazos River. They would move about half the distance in the daylight, then slow and work ahead more cautiously in the dark, the Indian scout One Hand Ready and Corporal Hoover leading the way.

Surprise was the only way to be sure the army could engage the hostiles. The Comanche didn't believe in having out a lot of scouts or lookouts. That was partly because the country was so vast and so flat and unbroken that a dust trail could be seen for ten miles in the daytime.

Canyon liked the night scouting missions, and he knew that all of the Indian fighting units should use the tactic, but they probably wouldn't.

They rode. Canyon was still sore from the last ride. It wasn't his usual form of transportation these days. But before they got back from this ride, he would be toughened up. He rode up front mostly with the corporal scout and Colonel Colton. Well before it got dark, the colonel was in a talking mood.

"Well, Canyon O'Grady, the last name has to be Irish. But where in the hell did you get the strange name of Canyon?"

"Happened because of another army, I'd say, Colonel. I was about to be born and my father told my mother that they would be leaving Ireland just ahead of the British constabulary. My mother was always reading books and looking at paintings of America. She wanted to give me a name that fit the breadth and spirit of America and so she decided on Canyon.

"The good Father Rearden would have none of that talk so he baptized me Michael Patrick O'Grady. My parents never call me anything but Canyon."

"So why was your father in trouble with the British?"

"Father was one of the founders of the Young Ireland Movement and a close friend of Fintan Lalor and Padraic Pearse. That alone was enough to have the British hard after him.

"I was born only a few weeks before my family fled the Emerald Isle. By that time they had a price on my father's head, but then the English have been putting prices on the Irish since Cromwell. Father brought his new family to America and I had a name that was a nod to yesterday and a welcome to tomorrow."

"Have you ever been back there? Did your father go back?"

"Twice. He took me along both times, partly to conceal who he was. We stayed for two years each time. He put me in the hands of a group of wise friars who pounded everything they knew into this visitor from America."

"Another question I've been wondering about. Most IGs don't go around with their own special horses. How in hell did you wrangle that?"

"My boss has some power and I guess you'd have to say that rank has its privileges. Besides, I'm not at home on another animal."

Darkness closed around them and they stopped for a quick meal. It was to be with fires, but closely concealed in dense brush and as little smoke as possible. Canyon went from fire to fire showing them how to find the driest wood that would make the least smoke.

One of the sergeants stared at him in surprise. "Sir, how come you're down here with the troops telling us this?"

"Sergeant, if we throw up as big a smoke as a company usually does, the Comanches in Colorado would know we were on the way. I'm trying to keep a dozen or so Comanche arrows out of my own hide, and out of yours."

The trooper laughed at that and Canyon continued on his rounds. Back at the colonel's small fire, O'Grady instructed the commander's orderly, who came along to do the cooking, in dry-wood fire making.

"Colonel Colton, if you're going to continue these night raids, I'd suggest you give your troopers some instruction in smokeless fires and in silent movement on and off their horses. It would also help if you'd set up a light saddle so your troops could move faster.

"Most trooper's saddle and gear weighs a hundred pounds. If you can cut twenty pounds off that, your animals will react well and your result could be an average six miles an hour instead of four. Just something to think about."

"O'Grady, just who the hell are you, anyway?"

"Just what I appear to be, Colonel. About the swift and silent travel? I've known some excellent Indian scouts. I've trained some of my men to use Indian skills and tactics. For instance, I could take a detail of ten men, strip down their gear to sixty pounds, not take any food, and do a five-day forced march making seventy-five miles a day.''

"Not possible. No rations?"

"No. Along with my detail would be three Indians, and they would be our hunters. We would live off the land, and live better than on salt pork and hardtack. It can be done, but it takes training and dedication by men and officers. I also taught some of my men to ride off the side of a horse exactly the way the Comanche do, and they could fire their revolvers under the horse's neck.''

"Be damned. You'll have to show me that sometime. That living off the land . . . what would your Indians find to eat out here?"

"Easy. Lots of animal life here. Jackrabbits would be the staple. They get big in Texas, can go to eight pounds so one jack will feed four men all day. Then there are squirrels, a few partridges, and always rattlesnake. For water we simply follow known streams or water holes.''

"Be damned. Might try that sometime, if you stick around to train those ten men and the Indians.''

They rode along in the darkness and Canyon felt the career officer's eyes watching him.

"O'Grady, I checked over that envelope you gave me from the president. It didn't have the usual marks and notes and creases on it a letter gets going through the usual chain-of-command army dispatch delivery. How did you get the letter?"

"Oh, that was easy. President Buchanan handed it to me himself and asked me to bring it to you.''

Colonel Colton frowned as he watched the young man beside him. He said a soft "Oh," and then tried to think it through. That simply meant that Canyon O'Grady must be much more than he seemed. Was he really from the IG's office, or was that simply an easy way to get him on the post to do whatever he was supposed to do here?

63

The colonel nodded and the touch of a smile came back. At least O'Grady wasn't there to sack him, or the president's letter would have done that. O'Grady's job was something else. He would find out soon enough. For now he had an engagement to plan against the damned Comanche. He would wait until he got there. As usual, the plan would depend on the situation and the terrain.

Three hours later they came to a spot selected for their assembly point. The troops would stay there until ready to move into position for the attack.

The officers and scouts and three sergeants met with the colonel.

"One Hand Ready will take us up to look over the terrain in a few minutes. It is now eleven P.M. We'll survey the situation and have our troops in position at five-thirty A.M. Lieutenant Emmery, you'll stay at the site here and be in charge until we return. All units will rest or sleep. Let's go."

The eight men moved quietly up the back of a gentle slope to a ridge line and looked down. They were about three hundred yards from the Brazos where it wound through a narrow valley. They could see the shadows of the tepee scattered along the ribbon of wetness. Here there was not a lot of brush and trees. Some of it must have been used as wood during many years of summer camps.

The colonel lay on the lip of the ridge looking down at the camp. Canyon was on one side and Captain Lancer on the other.

"Yes, looks familiar, Lancer. About like the last time. I'll bring half the company up on this side. You and Lieutenant Emmery come up the far side. When you get in position have One Hand Ready hoot like an owl. They should all still be sleeping by that time. We'll try for five-thirty to be at the point of attack."

"Spread our men out along the whole camp or take one section of it?" Captain Lancer asked.

"Yes, good point, Lancer. You take upstream and seal that end and spread about halfway down, but don't get too thin. I'll take the downstream end and seal it there and cover the lower half.

"We'll all fire four rounds into the tepees and then make our mounted charge. Our purpose here is to kill warriors and to destroy the camp. Any questions?"

There were no more, and the eight men turned and walked as silently as possible back to their assembly position about a half-mile from the camp. There were to be no fires and no lights, and they could see none as they came toward the sixty troopers.

It was midnight when Canyon checked his pocket watch with a stinker match under his blanket. He couldn't sleep. It would be another slaughter. Somehow he couldn't approve. True, the warriors were inhuman when it came to white captives, killing them, making them slaves, treating them like property or trash.

Yet the idea of streaming down from the sides of the little valley and catching the whole camp in a murderous cross fire of army rifle bullets did not seem like the right thing to do either. That was when Canyon discovered that he could never truly be a soldier. This was not one-on-one combat; this was slaughter.

He paced and worried and thought it through and paced again. At least he wouldn't fire his rifle into the tepees before the charge.

Canyon was still awake when the colonel's orderly came around to wake him. They left from the assembly-point camp at five o'clock and moved into their attack position and waited for the daylight. Canyon was with the colonel. The moon, which had been out bright and full, was now shrouded with dark clouds, which could mean rain. They could see only halfway into the valley, and not far enough to make out the tepees.

At five-thirty it was still too dark to see anything. The hooting of an owl came from the far ridge line, but Colonel Colton held up the attack. He wanted to see what he was shooting at.

Five minutes slid by, then another five, and the light began to gobble up the darkness. At a quarter-to-six it was light enough to see the river.

"Goddamn," Colonel Colton roared. "The bastards are gone."

It was true. Every tepee that had stood so strongly a few hours before had been taken down and was gone, or at least out of sight.

"Sound the charge," the colonel shouted to his bugler, who had been primed and ready.

The troopers, all mounted and waiting, stared into the empty valley, then swept down the sides following their sergeants when the bugle ordered them to.

Canyon grinned as he followed the colonel down the slope to the former campsite. The other half of Baker Company raced into the camping area and sat on their mounts waving their revolvers and feeling a little worthless just looking around.

Captain Lancer sent two men to the north and two to the south to scout out the trail of the fleeing Indians. He reported to the colonel and told him of his action.

"We'll know which way they went soon. Bound to be to the north and west toward the cliffs and the Staked Plains."

"Get One Hand Ready and track them," Colonel Colton screamed. "If they go that way, fire two shots. Ride!" The colonel slapped a riding crop against his blue pants leg. "Damn, damn, damn! How did they hear us?"

Canyon stepped down from Cormac and studied some drag marks on the dirt around the stream.

"Travois marks," he said to the colonel. But when he looked back at the officer, he was staring into the water, a soft smile on his face. He stepped down from his horse and tossed pebbles into the stream.

Canyon went toward him and the colonel turned. "Halston, there you are. Tell Mrs. Colton that dinner will be on the veranda tonight, will you? That's a good fellow." The colonel turned and threw two more stones into the creek.

From upstream came the sudden and sharp report of two revolver shots.

The colonel didn't seem to notice. He bent and put his hand in the stream, reacting to the coolness of the water and watching the riffles and the rocks.

Canyon walked up near him. "Sir," he said loudly. The man turned. "Colonel Colton, the captain has found out which way the Indians have escaped." Canyon said it forcefully, emphasizing each word.

For a moment James Henry Colton's face went blank, then he shivered and blinked rapidly. "Yes, I love a stream. Canyon, any word yet on those savages?"

"Yes, sir. Two shots just came from upstream. We better move the troops up that direction quickly."

"By God, yes! Bugler sound boots and saddles. Let's form into a column of fours and move upstream. We'll catch those damned hostiles yet."

The bugler blew the call and Canyon and the colonel galloped to the head of the column to the north and led the sixty troops at a trot upstream.

Canyon frowned as he looked at the regular-army colonel. The man had totally shut out the present; he had been in some world many years ago. Only a shock of Canyon's voice had brought him back. Was this what happened when he said his eyes had blacked out for a moment on that other patrol that Captain Lancer told him about?

7

Baker Company, Fourth Cavalry Regiment, galloped through the brush and the trees, out into the valley and upstream for a quarter of a mile before they caught up with the trackers. One Hand Ready was riding hard ahead, following the deep ruts of the travois, trying to catch the hostiles. The other scout, Corporal Hoover, reported to Colonel Colton.

"They left quick last night," he said. "Missed some things in the dark. Ain't like the Comanche to do that. Got damn scared that we was going to attack in the dark.

"Figure by the horse droppings that they've been gone for a good four hours. Must have known we were there around eleven o'clock or so. Could have been a hunter coming back or a medicine man out talking with the spirits. Takes two hours to strike camp and get moving."

"Can we catch them?" Colonel Colton asked, his voice angry, not at the corporal.

"No, sir. Not a chance. Already two travois have split off one due north, one south. Every mile or so they'll split off two more travois until every tepee in the camp is on a different course into the far country.

"Oh, we can find the individual woman driving the horse pulling all her family's worldly goods. But it'll be just her and the kids and the tepee and whatever food they've managed to get ready for winter."

"Where are the warriors?" Canyon asked.

"We'll be finding them soon. Usually they leave a rear guard, maybe four or five men, and any rifles they have will be there for an ambush to slow us down. The rest of them are probably near to the breaks that go up the cliff to the Staked Plains."

"Goddamn!"

"Yes, sir, I agree. I should have stayed as lookout on the camp. Takes them two hours to pack up to move. First thing I saw a tepee come down I could have fired three shots and we still could have hit them before they were ready to move. Warriors wouldn't leave without their families and their goods."

"Not your fault, Corporal. Go bring One Hand Ready back. If we find their rear guard, we'll hit it and try to wipe it out. Get moving."

The colonel at once ordered ten men out a hundred yards as flankers on both sides. If the main body ran into a rear guard, the flankers were to work silently forward and behind the hostiles and close in on them from the rear.

They rode for another hour. Corporal Hoover found One Hand Ready and brought him back. At the end of the hour, the colonel called a halt.

Corporal Hoover shook his head. "No rear guard, I guess, Colonel."

"I guess not, Hoover." It was almost eight A.M. "Let's go home, Captain Lancer. Take command of the return."

Cormac snorted softly and nuzzled O'Grady where he stood watching the troops do a to-the-rear and ride back the way they had come. Captain Lancer put two outriders on each side for security, sent three riders a quarter of a mile ahead, and left three as a rear guard a quarter of a mile behind, and the troops headed back the thirty miles for home.

Colonel Colton seemed more relaxed now that the

chance of an imminent battle was gone. He whacked the riding crop on his leg and looked at Canyon. "I suppose you'll put in your report that I failed to leave an observer at the Indian's campsite so I could know of any movement they might make."

"Hadn't planned on it, no."

"Good. That's one little problem I'll never have again. If I get an enemy force or camp in sight, I'll have at least three pairs of good eyes watching them until we attack."

"Now that sounds like a good idea, Colonel. We'll get them next time."

The column arrived at Fort Johnson a little after four that afternoon, tired, trail-dirty, and hungry. Major Westcott met them at the gate and welcomed them back. He looked first at Colonel Colton, then along the line, and found no dead or wounded. His gaze paused at one sergeant, who shook his head briefly but never looked at the major.

"Good to have you back, Colonel Colton," Major Westcott called. "Did you have any contact?"

"No," Colonel Colton said brusquely, stepped down from his horse, which was taken by an orderly. The colonel marched stiffly to his quarters, where his wife would have hot water waiting on the stove for his bath. Without a hot bath after every long ride he couldn't get out of bed the next morning. But no one knew that except his wife and his orderly.

Canyon went with the man assigned to handle his horse to the stables with Cormac, put the big palomino in a special stall, and saw that he was wiped down and then brushed. The golden mount got a double ration of oats, and only then did Canyon head for his own quarters.

By that time Sergeant O'Hallohan had heated up the

water he had been boiling for two hours, and had the round galvanized washtub ready for a bath.

Canyon thought about his revealing two or three minutes with Colonel Colton there beside the water when he threw rocks into the stream. The man had lost touch with reality. He had flashed back into an earlier, easier time. Why?

Just before that there had been the realization that the enemy had fled. The commander of the strike had made a mistake for all to see, and the strain of command must have surged up and been tremendous. His heart must have pounded furiously, his eyes flared, his whole system in a shock of pressures.

Canyon wanted to talk to Captain Lancer again about the time when the colonel said that he had the black spots in front of his eyes. What was happening just before that time?

O'Grady stripped and then sat down and folded his long legs in the small circular tub. It was the same-type tub the laundry women used to do the clothes in the wash building. But it was better than a sponge bath. He scrubbed off the trail dirt, even washed his hair, and when he left the tub, he shaved with glorious hot water the sergeant brought him.

By the time Canyon was shaved and dressed, O'Hallohan had supper ready: rice and beans in a chili mix a Mexican had taught the sergeant to make, and mashed potatoes and gravy and fresh-baked bread. Canyon knew he was eating a dozen times better than the troopers.

The army used the company-kitchen system. Each company cooked its own food in garrison. Cooks could be selected and changed at the company commander's will. None of the cooks had any training and the food they were given to use from the quartermaster was far from being tasteful or attractive. Often the food was barely fit to eat. At least O'Hallohan would eat well, which was one of the prime reasons for becoming an orderly to an officer.

A reasonable time after eating, Canyon started to head toward Captain Lancer's quarters, but stopped before he got to the door. Not the army way. Instead, he had O'Hallohan go over to the captain's residence and inform him that Colonel O'Grady wished to have a word with him.

Captain Lancer came back with the sergeant and saluted smartly. "Captain Lancer reporting to the colonel as ordered, sir!"

Canyon returned the salute and motioned to a chair in front of the unlit fireplace. It was getting chilly enough nights to need the fire soon. "Lancer, I wanted to talk to you about the time our friend had black spots in front of his eyes. Tell me again about the situation of command just before you noticed this condition."

"We had discovered our quarry, about fifty Comanche warriors, riding directly to us, so we waited in total concealment in the brush along a small stream and water hole. The order was given to hold fire until the colonel's command.

"I was near the colonel, and when the savages came within two hundred yards of us, I looked over at him. He didn't seem even to be looking at the approaching Comanches. I figured he was waiting until they got close enough that everyone could hit his target.

"At a hundred yards I looked at Colonel Colton again and it seemed like he was singing some little song. I couldn't catch the words. When the hostiles were within twenty yards, I gave the command to fire myself, and we punished the Comanche and turned them around and drove them back, then charged and chased them into the dirt."

"So, Captain Lancer, just before the black spots, would you say that the colonel was under great pressure of battle? That he was in a state of high anxiety as he waited for the battle to start?''

"Oh, yes, sir. It's a feeling we all have just before a battle. Especially it's high when waiting in an ambush situation. You're staring right at an enemy that you often never see out here. He's right there and you want to fire, but you can't. The officer who is holding the troops in check is experiencing ten times the stress that the men are.''

"In this case the officer with the stress and the anxious thoughts and the pressure and all of the worry of command was Colonel Colton?''

"Oh, yes, sir. That's absolutely true.'' The captain paused. "Sir, are you saying that the black spots could . . . could have been the result of all the stress and pressure?''

"I'm not sure yet, Captain. But let's say you're a brand-new captain and you've been sitting behind a desk in, say, supply procurement in Washington, D.C. You've been there for five years and just got your gold railroad tracks and you want some combat so you'll have a chance of getting to be a major. You come west and suddenly you're on a patrol against the Indians and the nearest you've been to even shooting at somebody was when you fired at a cardboard cutout of an Indian on the target range five years ago.

"Now you have sixty men to lead and take care of and command and you have to do it absolutely right or those men and you as well could very well wind up dead in the middle of Texas. Wouldn't you feel one hell of a lot of stress?''

"I'd be paralyzed, Colonel. On my first engagement against an Indian band, I was scared shitless. Only by sheer willpower did I lift my rifle and fire and lead my small patrol forward. Damn miracle any of us survived. But every time since then some of that stress and worry has flaked away. Now I know what I'm doing, what my men can do, and it's more a thinking situation now, not one of fear and pressure.''

"I'm wondering if Colonel Colton is feeling the same way. It looks like there could be a situation where instead of flaking away that worry and fear and pressure by repeated engagements with the hostiles, those emotions and stresses could build and multiply.''

Captain Lancer nodded. "I don't like the logical conclusions to this discussion, Colonel.''

"Neither do I, Captain, but if they are logical, all we have to do is find out if they are true, in this situation.''

"Oh, damn.''

The two men sat there for some time staring at the charcoal of a dead fire.

"You plan on talking with the colonel about this?''

"No, not yet. Not until I'm entirely satisfied that what I fear might be happening is actually taking place. I have another worry right now I think it's time I talked to you about. It also concerns the colonel.''

Briefly Canyon told Captain Lancer about the unknown trooper who came to him telling of the two officers talking about killing Colonel Colton on a patrol.

"My God! That's one fear every officer in combat has to wrestle with. His own men must be commanded, but they also must not learn to hate their officers. In today's army, it's all too easy for the enlisted men to fear and hate all officers. Why shouldn't they? They are often treated like animals. They get inferior food, inferior treatment, absolutely harsh and often unjust punishment, can't mix with officers, and woe to the enlisted who is caught dallying with an officer's wife or daughter.''

"Then you think that this threat is a real one?''

"Sounds like it is, if you can trust your informer.

The one way to squash that would be for you to order Colonel Colton not to go on any more patrols."

"I suggested the idea to him. He was adamant. He said the only way he won't go into the field is a direct order of the president or from his commanding general at Department Headquarters."

"There is another way."

"Yes, but I'm not about to relieve him of his command. That would be a stigma on his record and he'd have to retire. He wants to make general before he steps down."

"For the good of the service," Captain Lancer said softly.

"I know. The good of the whole. But right now the only thing he may be jeopardizing is his own life."

"What about the men in the patrol?"

"He's covered himself. He says he always takes you on his patrols. I think it's a subconscious way of protecting himself and making sure the men are not in any protracted danger. He knows if he goes down, you'll take over."

"Did something happen today out there on the patrol? Something I don't know about?"

"I really can't talk about that right now, Captain. I've told you too much already."

"You're compromised anyway, Colonel. In for a penny, in for a dollar. What do you have to lose?"

O'Grady told Captain Lancer about the dream world the colonel entered when they found out the band of Comanches had slipped away in the night.

"Sounds like almost the same thing that happened before. He must have tried to cover it up with the black-spots story." Captain Lancer stood and paced the room. "Damn, what are we supposed to do now, hold his hand when we're out on patrol? If it happened twice, we know damn well that it's going to happen

75

again. And the next time the colonel and half his men could be slaughtered."

Colonel O'Grady took a pint of whiskey from a cupboard and produced two small glasses and poured both half full. He handed one to Captain Lancer.

"Captain, I think I can trust you. I'm not sure of anyone else on the post I want to trust right now. There may be one more small problem at this fort. We have reports that unusually high numbers of army-issue rifles are turning up in the hands of hostiles. This number is far more than the savages have captured when defeating small units in battles and escaping with the weapons. Have you heard anything about this situation around here?"

"Nothing. I'll check the number of army weapons that have been surveyed and broken down for use as spare parts. There shouldn't be over one or two weapons a month in that category."

"I'd appreciate it."

Both men sipped at the whiskey.

After a while Captain Lancer looked at Canyon. "Colonel, I don't know what to say about our regimental commander. I'm just stumped. This is not my area of skills."

"Since you're going to be one of the officers with him on these missions, I want you to be especially alert just before an attack, or any other time of high stress for the colonel. If it looks like he is drifting off into another world, you take over command at once without seeming to, and do the right thing. You have the combat experience. If I'm nearby, I'll do the same.

"One more blackout or drifting off into another world by Colonel Colton will be enough to convince me we need to do something. At that point we'll figure out what it is.

"On the death threat, I have no idea why, other than

blind jealousy or the desire for a faster promotion. I don't know much about either of the majors on post.''

"Not a chance on Major Stanton. He's third in command, but a better man you'll never find. Major Westcott seems to be a true army officer, but he's a glad-hander. I don't know enough about him. He's been here about six months now.''

"The doctor," Canyon said. "It might be possible for the doctor to order the colonel to stay on post for some tests, some observation.''

"But what for, Colonel O'Grady? The commander would be suspicious at once. He wouldn't stand for it.''

"You're right. All we can do now is watch and wait, and hope we can catch anything untoward before it happens." As the captain walked to the door, Canyon touched his arm. "Remember, Lancer, this is all between you and me. Don't say a word of this even to your wife.''

Captain Lancer nodded and stepped outside.

8

It was well after midnight that same Saturday night, which had become Sunday morning, when Major Westcott and Lieutenant Hartsook rode due west away from Fort Johnson. They each carried a Spencer rifle, and Lieutenant Hartsook led a horse with two heavy bundles tied on its back.

They had left the paddock separately and met a quarter of a mile beyond the fort.

Hartsook was twitching in the saddle, grinning like a new bridegroom and laughing softly as they rode.

"Damn, it was like jumping over a log it was so easy. Got me those other five rifles in about ten minutes last night. Never saw men so eager to lose a weapon in my life."

"You know how we're going to do it?"

"Hell, yes, Major. I'm not an idiot."

"We're both smart enough on this one. I'll ride up first to the cottonwood and wait for Long Jack. You be close enough, but not too close. We want to do more business with Long Jack, but we aren't going to be robbed by him either."

"Sure as hell agree with that. Don't worry, I'm locked and loaded and ready for anything." He patted the Spencer repeating rifle in his saddle boot.

A half-hour later Major Westcott, without his shoulder boards on his jacket, rode up to the big cottonwood along the creek and stepped down and tied the packhorse, then waited.

Evidently Long Jack had gotten there first and had been watching. He stepped out from directly behind the cottonwood and laughed. "Hell, if I'd been a snake I'd have hit you three times. I see you got the goods."

"Long Jack, you're always a surprise. Of course we deliver on our promises. Let's check the gold first."

"Fair is fair," Long Jack said. His hand dropped to his side and for a moment Major Westcott wasn't sure if the Comanchero was going to draw or reach for the sack of gold.

He brought out the gold in two leather pouches. "My friend, seven hundred and fifty dollars of gold at twenty dollars and sixty-seven cents an ounce comes to two pounds, four and three-tenths ounces of gold. All duly weighed and certified. Oh, some of the gold is in double eagles."

"Didn't think Indians held with gold money."

"Don't. This one warrior stole the stuff from a ranch and didn't know what it was. I told him it was more woman's clay and he sold it to me for a pittance . . . but it's mine. Now it's yours."

Major Westcott checked inside the bags of gold using three stinker matches. It was gold all the way to the bottom, and one of the pouches had fifteen double eagles in it—three hundred dollars.

"Done, now you check the rifles. We want to do business with you again—say, in a month."

"Could happen," Long Jack said. He took his time opening the canvas-wrapped bundles on the horse and made sure that each of the rifles would fire. Then he wrapped them up again and started to put them back on the army mount.

"The horse doesn't go with the rifles," Major Westcott said sharply.

"Oh, sorry, 'course not. Just force of habit, I guess."

Major Westcott held out his hand. "If you can use some more rifles, plan on seeing us here again in a month. If that doesn't work out, stop by at the fort and ask directions. Leave your name and I'll see you at this same spot that evening at midnight."

"Sounds right to me, army man."

"I'll be leaving, then." Major Westcott hefted the two pouches of gold, turned, and walked into the blackness of the night.

An hour later the major and Lieutenant Hartsook sat in the major's bachelor quarters looking at the double eagles and the gold dust.

"The start of a fine new enterprise," Major Westcott said, clinking the gold coins in his hands. "We'll split the coins and the dust equally; that way we can spend some of the gold right away if we can find anywhere to buy something."

"That's going good, but what about our other little project, the demise of our dearest friend and colonel?" Hartsook asked.

"The patrol yesterday came up empty, so there went our first chance," the major said. "Don't worry, there'll be more. The way the old man is sending out his scouts, we should have at least one patrol a week bound to find Indian flesh. That means shooting, and that gives our man a chance."

"How much is this costing us?" Hartsook asked.

"Captain Philburton said he figured he can get the job done for a hundred dollars, twenty-five each. That is damn near a year's pay for the enlisted man and he goes on a long ride over the hill the next day."

"Be damn well worth it."

"Hey, he only refused to put you in for first lieutenant. He cost me a shot at lieutenant colonel."

"Yeah, fine, let's split the money and gold so I can get some sleep."

"Tomorrow's Sunday, light duty."

"Light, hell! My company is on rotation for the next company-sized scalping patrol. It could come tomorrow, who knows?"

Major Westcott chuckled. "What a sweet deal. We made our connection with the Comanchero. Once we get the colonel out of the way, we can sell him damn near half the fort before anybody knows. By that time you and me will be halfway to Mexico City with about fifty thousand in gold. We'll live like kings the rest of our lives down there."

Sunday was usually a quiet day around army posts. That was true at Camp Johnson, and Canyon used the time to catch up on his sleep and try to rethink the problems he was supposed to solve. It could be that Colonel Colton could work well in the army's scheme of things without his being a field-combat officer. But that was not for Canyon to decide.

He thought of going to see Captain Lancer on some pretext just to talk to his daughter, Cindy, but he pushed the idea aside. He did some more reading on his cavalry field manual just to be sure he wasn't tripped up anywhere along the line.

Monday morning he was back hard at work on his analysis of what information he had so far on the three troubles. The death threat worried him the most right now. How could he tie it down? He had absolutely nothing to go on except that the trooper "thought" the two men he overheard had been officers. It was impossible to dig them out without some clues.

About ten that morning, a knock sounded on the front door. He remembered that Sergeant O'Hallohan, his orderly, had gone to the fort's small store to buy some boot polish.

Canyon opened the door and found a woman standing there. She was dressed in a common print dress, wore a scarf over her head, and carried a laundry basket.

"Colonel, sir, you're on me list for laundry. Would you be needing any done this week?"

The woman must be one of the "suds" ladies, wife of an enlisted man assigned to do laundry for the officers and cleaning if they didn't have an orderly. The dress she wore was thin and tight across an ample bosom.

"Yes, I think I might. Would you step inside for a moment?"

"Yes, sir. I only come once a week, so you know it's on Monday and you can have your laundry all ready and waiting for me."

"I won't be here that long, but this is a good time to get caught up. What's your name?"

"Gert, Gert Jones. Wife to Sergeant Roger Jones."

"Oh, I see. Well, let me get my laundry for you." He put out his hand for the basket, but she held on to it.

"I've been in a bedroom or two, Colonel. Lead the way."

Canyon, a little self-consciously, pulled some of his used clothes out of a dresser drawer and dropped them in the basket.

"If'n you have anything on you want done, I can do it, too," Gert said. She grinned.

"Now, Mrs. Jones—"

"Call me Gert, and none of that Mrs. stuff. That don't bother me a whit."

The idea came as he was finding the last of his dirty socks. He smiled and looked up. "Gert, you must be in a lot of officer's quarters. You ever hear anything?"

"Now and then, a little bit. Know you're not our regular IG and everybody wonders why you're here."

"Partly I'm chasing rifles. You hear anything about army rifles getting into the wrong hands?"

"Like Comancheros? Been going on long as I been here, one or two a month, nothing big."

"Something big is going now. You hear anything about missing rifles, I'd appreciate it if you would tell me."

"Snitching on the officers. I like that."

"What about the enlisted?"

"My man could do some asking around, quiet. But it'll cost you. I might need some personal persuasion as well."

"What kind of persuasion, Gert?"

She grinned. Gert was maybe thirty, short, and a little heavy—comfortable, the army men would say. She was no beauty but had a curious appeal.

She walked to him, reached up, and pulled down his head and kissed his lips. When it ended she grinned. "A little friendly persuasion on your bed . . . if I can get in the mood." She stepped back and eyed him. "Canyon O'Grady, it is. A bit Irish. Don't worry, I told O'Hallohan you'd be busy for an hour or so. I'm not out of bounds. I'm the officers' woman, you know. But I ain't no whore. I got to be in the right mood, I do."

"If you were in the right mood, then later on you might be able to talk your man into helping me with the enlisted?"

"Might at that. A girl likes a little romancing." She looked at him. "My, you are a fine-looking man. Bet you have red hair on your chest and . . . down below. Right?"

"Maybe you'll find out, Gert." He bent and kissed her, seeing the flare in her eyes. He held the kiss and jammed his tongue into her mouth. She sighed, and when he let her go, she dropped on the bed, one hand at her forehead.

"Christ, nobody kissed me that way before. You're getting my jangles all a jingling here already." She patted the bed beside her and Canyon sat beside her, pushing his leg against hers.

"Try that again," she said, her eyes half-closed. He kissed her again. Her mouth was open, and he eased her back on the bed and came partway on top of her crushing one breast with his chest.

She moaned in delight, and when their lips parted, she let out a long breath. "Oh, yeah, you're all man, no doubt there. Love the way you smash me down."

His loins were on fire. The blaze burned brightly, stirring him. He left her lips and pulled her up so they both sat on the edge of the bed again. His lips moved to her breast and he breathed hotly into the fabric covering one, and she squirmed. Then he kissed the breast and she moaned.

He pulled the buttons open, spread back the cloth, and kissed the warm sweet flesh of her mound. Slowly he worked around it, up across the wide pink circle to the bud in its center. He licked it and swayed it back and forth and he could sense it filling with her hot blood, rising, stiffening.

He moved to the other breast and did the same there.

"Beautiful . . . that is so fine," Gert said. She yelped in delight, throwing back her head and squealing in pleasure as her breasts turned into twin mounts of fire.

Quickly then she pushed the dress off her shoulders so it fell to her waist. His hands caught her breasts which were set low on her chest, and he caressed them like they were two fine jewels.

"Seduce me slowly," Gert said.

He bent and his tongue drew a line of fire down from her breast to the rumpled dress at her waist. She lifted up and he pulled the dress down over her hips and it fell on the floor. She wore only soft cotton bloomers.

"My turn," Gert said. "Christ, I'm so hot now I don't know how I can wait." She pushed her hands over his crotch, found his hardness, and unbuttoned his fly. She worked her fingers inside. At once she found his manhood.

"Now, there's a good boy, so big and hard already. I think Gert excites you, Canyon O'Grady." She stroked him inside his pants, then worked him out and bent for a better look.

"Oh, God, he's beautiful!" She kissed the purple tip, then down the shaft and back up the other side. Her tongue licked him and she hummed softly as she did. When he was well-lathered, she slipped him into her mouth and sucked on him a minute, then bobbed up and down on him until he pushed her away.

"Not yet," he said.

Gert watched him from heavy, passion-filled eyes. She moved, going to her hands and knees, letting her big breasts swing down. "Chew me again," she said.

He pushed under her, his excitement rushing to meet hers. He centered under her hanging twins and licked and chewed and bit both of them until she yelped in delight.

"So damn good, Canyon!" She tore at his shirt, popping a button, pulling the cloth off him, and nuzzled the red hair on his chest. Then she jumped off the bed, her big breasts swinging as she pulled his boots off then his pants. Gert laughed softly as she eased down his short underwear and then he was naked. "Kiss my bloomers off," she said, dropping to the bed on her back.

Canyon hovered over her, then pulled the soft cotton down an inch at a time, kissing them lower. He aimed directly for her heartland and soon came to the dark swatch of tangled fur. He nosed through it and she trilled in excitement.

"God! No man has ever kissed me down there."

He pushed the cotton lower and lower until he could see the swollen redness of her.

"Oh, Christ! He's gonna do it." She shrieked the last and he didn't care who heard.

He nuzzled lower again and smelled the musk of her, the clinging perfume of her body and her red, moist nether lips. Canyon bent farther and kissed them.

"Oh, God . . . he's doing it!" Her whole body stiffened, then she trembled and roared and raced, and he felt her hips heaving up at him in a pounding dance. She spasmed and a high keening wail came from her, echoing around the quarters.

"Oh, yes. Oh, yes. Yes! Yes! Yes! Oh, oh, oh, oh. Christ, I'm gonna die! Ummmmmmmmm. Oh, yes. Daaaaaaaaaaaaam." Then he no longer could make out any words as she whimpered and wailed and moaned until at last she tapered off and caught his head with her hands and hugged him to her round little belly.

He lifted away from her and stripped the bloomers off her legs and all the time his ears were pounding with the roaring of a sea of blood, his own superheated body fluid.

Canyon watched her face. Gert's eyes opened and they worshiped him.

"Anything," she said softly. "Anyway you want me, anyplace. Just push it into me now before I die." She pulled him over her, lifted her legs over his form, and locked them behind his back. Canyon nudged toward her heartland. She caught him and guided his missile until it hit the wet, ready lips and plunged inward.

"Oh, God! I'm in heaven . . . so good . . . don't ever leave." Then she wailed and shouted and lifted her hips to meet his. They worked against each other and she built and built.

Canyon felt his own pressure mounting, felt as if he wanted to blow the roof off with one mighty thrust, and then Gert roared over the top before him, shattering her whole body, jerking and shivering and spasming again and again.

Canyon got into the spirit and the flesh of it and knew he couldn't stop. He jolted with her a dozen times, then rode her through one last mighty spasming that ended with her screech of animal satisfaction just before he collapsed on top of her and they lay there sweating and panting like a pair of steam engines.

Ten minutes later she moved and he lifted away from her.

"I got some damn laundry to do or I won't get it dry by tonight," she said.

"Now, you hear anything about rifles missing around the barracks?" Canyon asked.

"My man said something about it last night. Somebody came to his barracks and later two rifles were 'lost.' The men said they lost them on patrols but were afraid to tell."

"Which means they sold them to somebody?"

"Hell, yes. Sold them to somebody who sells them to the fucking Comanches, who shoot back at the guys who sold them."

They sat up on the edge of the bed.

He cupped one of her heavy breasts with one hand. "Can you find out which company's men lost those rifles?"

"Yes, tonight. My man probably knows, I didn't think it was important."

"It might not be to him, but you find out for me, tonight if you can. Right now it's damn important." He paused. "Oh, also find out who they sold the rifles to. I'd like a name and rank if possible."

He lifted away from her, reached in his pocket, and took out a ten-dollar gold eagle. "This is on my account. I may need to know some other things, other names."

"Sweetheart, whatever you need to know, me and my man will find out, and nobody will know about it. My Roger may drink a little, but he is good at talking." She bounced off the bed and slipped on her bloomers and her dress.

She stood there with the basket watching him. "Jesus I like to see you all bare-assed naked. You've got muscles I never knew a man had, and, Christ, do you know how to use them. I'll bring something back tonight, some laundry, and have the information you want. If not, first thing in the morning." She turned and hurried to the door. "Oh, forgot to tell you. Laundry is a dollar a week. You can afford it." She winked, shook her breasts at him, and hurried out of the room.

Canyon O'Grady chuckled a moment, then buttoned his fly and went to the small desk. He made some notes about what the woman had said and stared at them. It was strange where a thread of a lead might turn up. Now, if it just panned out, he'd be more than pleased.

He took out the sheet of paper about the kill threat on the colonel. The more he stared at the threat as he knew it, the less he came up with a way how to find the culprits. He had talked with almost all of the officers now in the regiment. At first glance, none of them seemed hateful enough to even think about shooting their commanding officer.

He thought about Gert. He had heard about the laundry-women whores that the army condoned. There were always enough women married to enlisted men on any camp so a select number could be utilized as prostitutes for the soldiers. Especially on posts such as this one, with no benefit of a local town for the men.

In the same fashion two or three of the best of the ladies were for "officers only." In some cases the husbands of the women were lowbrow, poor soldiers hardput to stay in the army. But if their wives were good enough in bed, the officers often tolerated an otherwise unacceptable level of soldiering by the husbands.

O'Grady pushed that line of thinking away and concentrated on his three problems. He was making the most progress on the colonel's situation. At least he had a good lead there that might prove to be the correct one, and the solution to the problem wouldn't be difficult. The president had given Canyon another sealed envelope with Colonel Colton's name on it and told him to give it to the colonel once Canyon knew that Colton had made his decision. That envelope could contain a solution to the colonel's situation.

But the other two were tougher . . . the death threat the worst. What in the hell did he do next trying to track that down?

9

Before noon that Monday, Canyon walked into Regimental HQ and looked at the sergeant major at his desk near the front of the big room.

"The colonel?" Canyon asked.

"Sir, he's been talking to Major Westcott for quite a while now. Not a friendly discussion."

"Goddammit, no!"

They both heard the colonel's angry voice come through the closed door to his office.

"He say anything about not being disturbed?"

"No, sir."

Canyon went to the door, pushed it open, and walked in as if there had been no big fight. He grinned at Major Westcott, who glared back at him.

Colonel Colton stared out the window, his back to them.

"I told you no, Major," Colonel Colton said, a tiredness creeping into his voice.

"It's something we should discuss, Colonel. You know damn well that I'm right on this. I'll be back later this afternoon." Major Westcott turned and walked quickly out of the room, giving Canyon an angry look as he left.

Colonel Colton kept looking out the window. He shivered once, then again before he turned around. For just a moment Canyon saw the same far-off look in the colonel's eyes that he had seen out on patrol.

Slowly it faded and the commander lifted his brows and slumped in the big chair behind his desk.

"I don't know why I let him get me upset. Sometimes it seems to me that he's baiting me about things not really important. Like now. He keeps pushing and pushing."

"Wants your job, Colton. It's printed all over him in large type."

"He's only a major. He doesn't have a chance. Even if I got promoted and moved out of here, they would send in a new commander, at least a light colonel."

"Has he tried for a promotion through you?"

"Yes, of course. He's only been a major for two years. He came up quickly, but he should know it takes at least six years from major to light colonel these days. Damn slow. But if we have that war with the South . . ." The colonel looked at Canyon quickly. "You're from Washington. What's the talk about a war? If the South goes ahead and secedes, then Congress will have to declare war to preserve the Union, right?"

Canyon nodded. "That seems to be the feeling. The hope is that it's a bluff and the president's policy of states determination slave or free will hold the South."

"But it won't! Damn, if we get into it with the South, this little army of ours is going to explode. What do we have now? About twenty thousand men. Hell, we could go to two million. Know how many generals we'll need for a force of two million?"

"A whole bunch, Colonel. You want to be one of them?"

"Hell, I'll piss in my soup for a year to get my stars. But I figure you know that."

"Just one problem, Colonel. A man has to be alive to be promoted to brigadier general, even brevetted."

"So?"

"Colonel, I've had a report of a death threat against

91

you. I didn't want to tell you, but I've decided now is the time. Yes, it was anonymous, a voice in the shadows, an enlisted man who says he heard two officers talking in the stable one night when they thought they were alone. But who else could he tell but an IG?''

"Rubbish. Every officer in the army has heard that sort of threat against himself.''

"Not this way. The enlisted man was so frightened he could hardly talk. I'm taking it seriously. Their plan was to make it appear as though you had been shot by the hostiles during a fight with the Indians.''

"Bastards! Something like that could work and nobody could be pinned down.''

"That's why, Colonel, I'm requesting that you not go on any more attacks on the Comanches.''

Colonel Colton walked to the window again and stared at the parade ground. "Goddamn! I know how those promotion boards work. Sat on enough of them myself. 'Look at this captain,' they say. 'He's only been on two shooting raids against the Indians and he wants us to make him a major. Needs more combat, more action. We want men who know the field.' ''

He gave a big sigh and turned to Canyon. "Hell, might not make any difference if we do have a war. They won't even look at service records. They'll need colonels and generals to head up divisions and armies. Need twenty or thirty new ones almost overnight.''

He came back and sat in the chair, his back ramrod-straight now. His brown eyes snapping under the thick brows that met in the middle. He scowled at Canyon. "Hell, I'll consider not going out, that good enough for you, O'Grady?''

"And the rifle slug that's fired at you will 'consider' blowing your brains out, Colonel. Is that good enough for you? I've got a problem here. Of course, if I don't help keep you alive, my problem is solved easy. But I don't want it done that way." Canyon grinned. "Hell, if I let you die, I might never make general either."

Colonel Colton shook his head. "Won't work anymore with me, O'Grady. You're not U.S. Army. I know it. Took me a couple of days to figure it out. You're not with the IG. No IG inspector would ever have direct access to the president. No inspector would ever hand-carry a letter from the president himself to someone in the field.

"I'm not sure exactly who you are, or why President Buchanan sent you here, but one thing is certain: the president is concerned about me or you wouldn't be here. Don't try to feed me any more horse turds for breakfast, O'Grady. You can fool these other jaspers all you want to. Hell, you don't even know how to salute properly."

Canyon watched the fort commander, then nodded. "Colonel Colton, you can believe anything you want to. I won't comment on it. But I know for damned certain that anytime you go on an armed patrol against the Comanches, you are putting your life at risk. You know there is one way I can prevent you from going out there anymore."

"Just one, relieve me of my command for cause."

"And that would end your military career and you'd never get that star. As an IG, and with the president's personal backing, I have the power to set you down. I wanted to be sure you understand that."

"Yes, O'Grady, I know you must have the authorization. I appreciate that. But I'm a career officer. That's something you don't know one goddamned thing about. I've got to do what I think is right, and that means smashing those Comanches every chance I get. I not only need the credits in my personnel file, I need the experience of leading troops in battle. That's because I know we're going to have a war, and damn soon. I know that I'll be promoted to general and soon get two stars, and I damn well need the combat experience right now so I don't slaughter hundreds of my men one or two years from now. Can you understand that, O'Grady?''

Canyon nodded. "Yes, I do understand. It's a chance, a gamble, but even though you're not sure you can win, you want to try to fill that inside straight.'' He paced the room, looked out the window, then swore softly and made another circuit of the room.

"All right, Colonel. One more damned patrol. Maybe I can stop these guys before they get to it. I hope. If not, the next gamble you take will be one of life and death. I want you to know that.''

Colonel Colton laughed. "I'm delighted. At least if I take a bullet, it will be in the field with a revolver in my hand screaming at the damned savages. You see, you've given me no choice, no alternative. If I refuse to stop going in the field and exposing myself, you'll put me down by relieving me of my command. Which will kill my army career.

"If you let me go into the field, I stand the chance of getting my head blown off from some trooper behind me. Oh, yes, it wouldn't be an officer who did it. They would hire somebody for two or three hundred dollars to do the job, then he'd be riding hard as soon as he could to desert with his blood money. This is not a new problem or a new scenario. It's been happening to officers and leaders since Cain and Abel. Remember that Julius Caesar was stabbed to death by his friends.''

"I'm trying my damnedest not to let that happen to you, Colonel Colton. Do you have your night-search scouts out right now?''

"Two pair of them, in fact. I like to get in one good fight with the Comanches every week. It's starting to make them think about moving farther out, maybe all the way up to the Staked Plains. If I can force them to move that far, this fort will have done its job.''

''Colonel, if you do go on another patrol, I want you to promise me that you'll keep well to the rear of the action and keep both your eyes watching your back. If anybody is going to try to shoot you, it will surely come from behind you.''

''Won't happen, I'm convinced of that. Now, how would you like to stop by at my quarters for lunch?''

''I would, Colonel, but O'Hallohan has my noon food all ready for me.'' He walked to the door. ''Remember, Colonel Colton, cover your rear and your flanks at all times.''

Canyon thought about it during his lunch. O'Hallohan had cooked up some stew with three vegetables and potatoes and lots of cut-up beef. They must have slaughtered another steer for the officers' tables.

He couldn't think of any other way to deal with Colonel Colton. Right now he wished that he knew what was in that second letter the president had given him to deliver to Colton, after any decision was made on his fitness. What a hell of a job. It was like being the judge and sentencing a man to death. That's what retirement would be for the colonel. He lived and breathed and bred army life.

Colonel Colton accepted the chance of sudden death or disabling injury every time he rode on a fighting patrol. That was living too close to the edge of death to suit O'Grady. Hell, a shoot-out now and then wasn't so bad, at least you controlled your own destiny. But to have some Comanche lie in wait and blow your brains out with a sniper's shot from ambush was playing a dice game of life and death that you had no way of influencing.

Someone knocked on the door and O'Hallohan answered it. He came back directly. ''Sir, Miss Lancer's at the door and she would like a word with you. She can't come in, of course."

Canyon grinned, thanked the sergeant, and went to the door. He stepped outside in the autumn air and smiled at the pretty, dark-haired girl. "Well, this is a surprise, Miss Lancer."

She smiled. "My father wants to know if it would be all right if he could come over and see you for a moment, or at a time you suggest." She smiled. "That's exactly the way he told me to ask you."

"I'd much rather talk to you," Canyon said, remembering the satin thighs, the excited little wiggle of her bottom.

"Sweet, wonderful Canyon, I'd much rather kiss you than talk," she said, her glance darting around to see if anyone could hear her soft words. No one could.

"Now, there is a fine idea. We'll have to see what we can arrange. Tell your father that I'll be here for the next hour and that that would be a most convenient time for me."

"Oh. Darn, I lost my bet with myself that you'd say, 'Tell the captain to get his ass over here right now,' or something like that." She laughed softly and reached out and touched his hands.

Canyon wanted to grab her and pull her inside and take her at once to his bed. Instead, he smiled. "You really win, because that's what I was thinking."

Cindy Lancer smiled. "I wish I could come inside for just a minute, but with three officers' wives watching, that would be my ticket back to Chicago. Come to think of it, that might not be a bad plan. It would get me out of here." But she turned, looked back over her shoulder, and winked at him, then she hurried off toward her father's quarters.

Canyon went back inside, asked for two cups of coffee and warm cinnamon rolls as soon as the captain arrived. Then he went back to his desk and pushed the three piles of papers into better order and then tried to figure out how he would go about hiring someone to shoot the colonel if he were doing it.

First he'd have to pick the right man, someone who wouldn't mind doing the job, wouldn't mind deserting the army, and one who might have been in trouble before.

It might be someone with chevrons or without. Canyon had been surprised that an enlisted man's rank was strictly up to the local commander. A sergeant in one company would tend to stay there for his whole hitch or career. If he was transferred to another unit, he would at once lose his stripes and be a private again. For that reason alone any man with chevrons tried to stay within his unit. It was the same all across the army.

But men in trouble would be on record. A good job for Lancer. About that time the captain knocked on the door and O'Hallohan let him inside.

The captain started to salute and Canyon waved him off.

"Sit down, Lancer. What have you found out?"

"I was checking on surveyed weapons, especially rifles. Usually about one a month goes down in a unit like this. The regiment had eleven surveyed the last month. I asked the quartermaster officer Lieutenant Fay about them and he shrugged. Said he left most of that kind of matter up to his quartermaster sergeant.

"We talked with him and this Sergeant Zigler said the eleven rifles had been classified as unrepairable due to major problems, and all had been broken down by the armorer and the parts kept in his various drawers and bins and baskets for use as spare parts. The armorer was not in when I was there. It seems all according to regulations."

"Yes, seems to be. Only what if the rifles that were surveyed were not that bad and had been repaired and made available to the person who sold them to the Comanchero?''

"Highly illegal, against regulation, with severe penalties for the culprit.''

"Such as ten years in a federal prison. Captain Lancer, I strongly suggest you move swiftly and carefully to see if you can tie down any more names and facts about this. If the armorer is a cog in the gun-selling machinery, we should be able to sweat the truth from him by giving him immunity to any punishment.''

"It's worth a try. What about the other two situations?''

"We were lucky on that last patrol. If there had been a fight with the Comanche, we might not have a post commander by now. I talked with him again. I told him of the death threat, but he said it was a good way to die. I also told him that if he insisted on going on the fighting patrols, I have the power to relieve him of his command. He said to die on a patrol would be better than being relieved, because both would end his military career. He thinks there's a big war coming up and he wants to be in it as a brigadier general.''

"If he lives through this, he probably will make it.''

"The damn death threat is my biggest worry, Captain Lancer. Do you have any idea how to dig into it?''

"Catch them in the act.''

"Which could be deadly. Is there a list kept of the enlisted who have been court-martialed, stripped of rank, or rowdy, malcontents, that sort of thing?''

"Absolutely. Usually company commanders keep a surprisingly complete list.''

"That's only twelve companies. I want you to check those companies and see what you can find. Any man who might be a logical candidate for a killing job and a quick desertion. Have the list of men for me by suppertime. Then, whenever a troop goes out on a killing patrol with the colonel, we'll leave anyone on that list, in that company, in the barracks.''

"Could work, Colonel. I'll get right on it. We could also watch for those men showing up as volunteers to go on such a mission. Yes, we might have a way to slow them down, whoever the hell they are, without even knowing who the hell they are.''

"Let's hope so. Until we come up with something else, a man's life hangs in the balance.''

10

It was a routine sweep patrol, one of those sent out weekly by the fort to check on the surrounding territory and watch for any dust trails of any large Indian movements. The assignment was to ride a proscribed route in a large triangle from Dry Wells to Burnt Arroyo and back to the fort.

The triangle would measure about sixty miles on the three-day ride. The group of six riders, a corporal, and Lieutenant Hartsook was not designed as a fighting unit. Their mission was to observe, not make contact with any seen hostile, and ride back and report any sign of Comanche, either moving or camped.

Hartsook had been on the same route four times now and it was routine. He took his harmonica along and practiced well out of hearing of the men. They moved the twenty miles to Dry Wells on the first day and camped under a straggly old cottonwood that was slowly dying for lack of water. Its deep roots sucked up whatever runoff moisture there was during the spring rains and a bit of water from the winter snow. Hartsook gave the big tree another five years with luck.

He thought of the $375 back in the deepest hidden part of his dresser, and grinned. Soon he would be a rich man and he could resign his commission and go into business for himself. He had always liked Santa Fe. It was growing and a natural business center. He would do fine there. The army had always been second choice for him.

The next day his patrol of eight operated on the usual cavalry schedule. They hadn't brought a bugler along and Hartsook woke up the corporal, who roused the men promptly at 4:45 A.M. That was first call and the men grumbled out of their blankets and got in motion.

At 4:55 A.M. it was reveille and stable call. At this time the men came to order, saddled their mounts, and got ready to travel.

At 5:00 A.M. sharp was mess call. The men had half an hour to prepare and eat their breakfast. Fires were allowed on this trip and the issue salt pork was boiled and roasted and fried over the fire usually in an over-size tin cup almost every cavalry man had. It was not regulation and bought at the sutler's store. The hard-tack was often soaked in the salt-pork juices and mashed up so it could be eaten.

At 5:30 came general call. Now the men struck camp. They had not even brought along their shelter halves, so it was a quick job to get everything stowed on board their mounts and ready to travel.

At 5:45 was boots and saddle call. Now the men mounted their horses. Ten minutes later the troops fell in to their normal column of march, and when it was in order, the unit moved out no later than 6:00 A.M. sharp.

They had ridden for three hours, and the men were getting tired and hot and cursing the blazing sun, which even in the end part of September was boiling hot. There was no water here for another ten miles, so the men slumped in their saddles and tried to tough it out.

Most of them tried to think of something pleasant. One remembered his last night with Sally. She was one of the suds women who would do anything he could think of for two dollars. He could only afford her once a month, but she was worth it. Damn, he didn't know a woman could bend the way she did.

The first arrow slammed into the side of Lieutenant Hartsook's big black mare before anyone saw a hostile. Then the Indians screamed and boiled up out of an arroyo waving their rifles and lances. Thirty Comanche warriors hurtled down on the eight blue-clad cavalry troopers, who hastily drew their revolvers and tried to make a fight of it.

"Dismount and take cover," Lieutenant Hartsook screamed. Just as he was dropping off his mount, a Comanche arrow with an inch wide metal man-killer point sliced into his side. The arrow point ripped through his blue shirt and parted two ribs before it drove halfway into the officer's heart. He slumped under the black mare's feet and didn't feel a thing as she shied away, then snorted and galloped away from the strange and terrible noise the Comanches made.

One of the blue-coats didn't dismount. He saw the overwhelming force of Comanche warriors, all mounted and heavily armed, and he turned to make a strategic withdrawal.

A screeching warrior with his face painted yellow and red stormed after the galloping private. The Comanche on his dessert-bred and -trained Indian pony had the advantage. The warrior guided the war horse with his legs and knees, and the speed of the wiry animal quickly caught up with the blue-shirted trooper.

The warrior surged forward and rammed his ten-foot lance ahead sharply. The four-inch-wide and six-inch-long steel point on the lance stabbed through the private's back and sliced all the way through his chest as the Comanche let out a war cry to inform his companions that he had made a clean kill.

Behind him, the rest of the warriors methodically butchered the remaining troopers still alive.

The corporal killed a warrior with a shot in his face from two feet away. He cocked his pistol and whirled to his rear and shot another savage with a lifted war ax. But before he could turn again two man-kill arrows sliced into his body and he sighed and turned to see a war pony riding him down. He died before the heavy hooves cut through his chest.

The warrior chief sat on his spotted war pony and nodded. It was good. The blue-shirts were all dead. Only one horse got away, the big black mare the leader had ridden. The rest had been captured easily. Seven horses! A good start on this raid.

He watched as his men methodically stripped the bodies bare. The cloth could be used by their women. Each rifle and revolver had been claimed by the individual who captured it. Every bit of the troopers' clothing and equipment was taken away. It would all be used, especially the treasured rifles. Eight of them! Walks Fast's band was especially fortunate.

Now began the ritualistic slashing and mutilation of the enemy. It had to be done. Now that the enemy was defeated in this life, there was still a chance that he would attack again when both were in the spirit world. If the bodies were cut and sliced and slashed and broken in this life, then they would bear the same damage in the spirit world and it would be much easier for the Comanche to defeat them again.

They took scalps, and then, less than fifteen minutes after the first arrow had been fired, the Walks Fast band was on its way south, south to Mexico.

Walks Fast smiled as they rode. It was to be a quick raid, so they had brought along no women to cook. They would eat from their food skins, pemmican and jerky. They could move sixty miles the first day and seventy miles the second. Soon they would be in Mexico and he knew that the hunting would be good.

He worried a moment about the escaped horse. She had been a fine big mare. There was a chance she would move back to the mud houses where the blue-coats lived. But that was not a worry. The blue-coats would be missed sooner or later anyway.

Walks Fast would not worry about that. He wanted

to think about the raids coming up. He was looking for a new Spanish woman, one to add to his tepee of two wives. The Spanish women bred like rabbits, everyone knew. Yes. A good Mexican woman would give him three sons.

Walks Fast turned the band of thirty warriors slightly more toward where the sun is born, and rode harder.

The big black mare that Lieutenant Hartsook had ridden walked back into Fort Johnson late that afternoon. She was bleeding from the arrow that still stuck from her left side just behind the saddle.

The mare walked directly to the stables without the formality of going in the front gate. The stable sergeant found her standing there, head down, and hurried her to the Regimental HQ. He knew who had ridden out on the horse the day before.

By the time the sergeant walked the horse to the headquarters there were thirty troopers following him. He ran inside and four officers came boiling out of the building.

Colonel Colton stared at the mount a moment.

"You said Lieutenant Hartsook rode out yesterday morning on this animal?"

"Yes, sir, Colonel. The lieutenant almost never rides nowhere without his Black Belle."

"That patrol is wiped out or in desperate trouble. Major Westcott, call out the standby company. We'll be riding in ten minutes. Move them!"

Everyone began running. Canyon ran to the stables and saddled a surprised Cormac, who nuzzled him for an apple and, when he got none, gave a little toss of his head as if it didn't matter.

Back at the headquarters building, Major Westcott talked to the colonel.

"It'll be dark in three hours. You can't hope to find them before dark."

"Right, Major. Bring along four lanterns full of kerosene. Where is Fox Company? Let's get moving, gentlemen!''

When they rode away from Fort Johnson, Canyon checked his pocket watch. It had been exactly nine minutes and forty-five seconds since Colonel Colton ordered the march.

They had been issued no rations. One Hand Ready and three more Indian scouts rode with them. A half-mile out of the fort the four Indians took off on their own.

Colonel Colton waved Canyon up beside him.

''The sweep patrol was on a routine run. They went out to Dry Wells northwest of here the first day. This is the second day, so they would be heading nearly due south of there toward Burnt Arroyo. If we ride west, we should be able to cut their trail out somewhere from fourteen to sixteen miles. Set the pace, Colonel. Let's see how quickly you can get these sixty men to that point.''

Canyon moved the steady four-mile-an-hour walk into a canter that would eat up nearly six miles in an hour. He kept them on that rate for a half-hour, then dropped to a walk a little faster than four. There had been no horses drop out or no complaints from the sergeants.

Fifteen minutes of walking and he lifted the horses to a trot, which could cover six and a half miles in an hour. Again after a half-hour he let the animals breeze back to a walk. They held that pace for half an hour.

''How far have we come, Colonel O'Grady?'' Colonel Colton asked.

''Between ten and eleven miles. Is there any landmark out here that we can use to figure out where the southerly route is the patrol would have taken?''

''Yes. Out of Dry Wells the route leads down a gentle, wide, shallow valley, then over a small ridge and down the other side. If they rode two hours, they should be about a third of the way down that far ridge. The ridge will be maybe four miles to our right.''

"What about Captain Quinlin? Has he been out here recently?" Canyon asked.

They called the captain up from the front of his company and he nodded.

"Yes, sir. I did this sweep about a week ago. The ridge should be to our right. We're what, about eleven miles out? If so that looks like the ridge over there about two miles."

They angled the line of march toward the ridge. A half-mile before they got there, One Hand Ready rode up and held up his arm and the officers stopped the march.

"We find tracks, eight army mounts come down ridge, head south."

"We should angle back due west?" Colonel Colton asked.

One Hand shook his head and pointed southwest.

They rode.

An hour later just before the beginnings of dusk, they cut the trail and the column moved to a trot and headed due south. They came over a small rise and found the bodies fifty yards ahead in the open.

"There's no rush now," Colonel Colton said softly.

The officers examined each of the eight bodies, then gave orders to wrap them in blankets and tie them securely. Then a body was put across the neck of each of the officers' and noncoms' horses and the detail headed for home.

Canyon was appalled by the mutilation of the bodies. He had heard that it happened, and he knew why. Still, seeing it in person was much worse than he had imagined.

They rode two hours, then came to a fire ahead, and when they arrived, they found two of the Indian scouts roasting rabbits over the fires. They were big jackrabbits, seven to eight pounds each. There were eight of the jacks roasting or already done. The troops stopped, unloaded their bodies, and rested. The rabbits were assigned by squads, with one of the big jacks for eight men.

Canyon pulled a rear leg off one of the cooked carcasses and sat down to chew his fill.

"Damn good idea, Canyon, living off the land. Not sure we could do it for every meal for long, but it sure as hell worked this time."

"Where's One Hand?"

"He and the other scout went down the hostiles' trail, making sure where they're heading. They have lanterns. When they're sure the Comanches are heading for Mexico, they'll come and tell us."

"What are your plans after that, Colonel Colton?" Canyon asked.

"I don't like losing seven men and an officer, O'Grady. We'll keep out low-profile patrols across a twenty-mile line along here, east to west. When the bastards come back from Mexico, we'll be able to see them ten miles off and have enough time to gather a blocking force. Then we'll get some satisfaction for losing eight good men."

"How will you time it?"

"I figure they'll need one more day to get to Mexico. They'll spend two days there and need one day to get back here. On the fourth day from now, I'll have two hundred men spread out across these twenty miles. The fourth day we'll be ready for them in our defense line. When we see the dust trail from the heathens coming, we start to ride. Our people will move slowly, making no dust, and converge on the spot along that line where the hostiles will be ambushed. I plan on hitting them with at least two hundred men and not letting a single damned Comanche get away."

They did not hurry on their night ride back to the fort. They arrived just before ten o'clock and the wife of one of the dead men had to be led away screaming in rage and pain at her loss.

Captain Lancer met the party, saw the bad news, and waited until Canyon was alone walking back from the stable, where he had watched a trooper brush down Cormac and give the big stallion his ration of oats.

"Rough trip."

"True. Rougher for those who got caught. Scouts said a party of about thirty warriors, no women."

"Mexican raid?"

"Looks like it. You find out anything?"

Captain Lancer grinned. "Sure as hell did. I found the armorer. He's Corporal Grenoble, good at his work. When I pointed out how many rifles had been surveyed out, he was surprised. He said he only stripped down two last month. Both of them were wrecks, and he got little from them he could save for spare parts.

"When I said eleven showed on his report, he got wide-eyed and started to shake and at last he gave me a name. He said he was told by an officer to sign the sheets for tear down. The corporal said the officer told him if he mentioned a word of this to anybody, the corporal could figure on being torn apart by two horses some dark night."

"So what made him talk? You torture him, Lancer?"

"Almost had to. Then we heard about that sweep patrol and the horse coming back with the arrow. Oh, I have a name of an officer who probably was selling rifles to the Indians, but it doesn't do us a damn bit of good.

"The officer leading that patrol was Lieutenant Hartsook. He's also the one who forced the corporal to sign the survey forms on those eleven rifles."

"Oh, damn."

"As soon as I found out there was a chance the patrol had been wiped out, I put a guard on the lieutenant's door, and tonight they set a special guard post on the door so no one can go in or out of his bachelor quarters.''

"Good, good. We'll check out his place tomorrow."

They stopped outside Canyon's quarters. "Come in for a drink."

"I already had one."

"Have another one."

It was well after midnight and the bottle's level was seriously lowered when Canyon had an idea.

"A second lieutenant didn't do this all by himself. He had some help, or more likely he was helping somebody else. Find out who Hartsook drank with, who he gambled with. There has to be some connection."

Captain Lancer snapped his fingers. "Poker party. Four guys play poker once a week, every Thursday night. I can find out. One of them was Hartsook, another one is Captain Erin Delaney. Two more. I'll find out. They asked me to play once, but I'm no good at poker and begged off."

"Yes, that's a start. Dig into it for me, but don't let on why."

"Right, I've got nothing else to do."

"Good way to make major."

"True. Oh, here's something else for you." Captain Lancer took out an envelope and handed it to the colonel. "Names of bad asses in the ranks. Top three men in each of the twelve companies who have had the most court-martials, the most fights, and been busted the most times. I got to get home or I'll get skinned."

"Just tell her that you were obeying orders and got a little drunk."

"Hell, yes, my wife will understand . . . with a skillet off my head." Captain Lancer grinned and hurried out the door to his quarters three doors down.

11

"Three-handed poker is a stupid game," Captain Lewis Philburton said as the three men sat around the kitchen table in Major Westcott's quarters.

"That's why we're not playing the game, but it has to look as if we are, if anybody drops by," Major Westcott said sharply.

Captain Delaney looked at him. "All right, I'm sorry. We're all a bit touchy right now. We lost Hartsook and nobody is happy about it. At least his going doesn't hurt our major plan. Everything is in place. We just haven't had a contact patrol lately."

Westcott looked over at Philburton. "Everything is in place isn't it, Captain?"

"Absolutely. The next patrol that goes out, my man goes along by hook or crook. I hear ambush-spotters will be riding out first thing in the morning on a line stretching fifteen miles across the plains. Is that right?"

"Damn close. We're stretching a fence of lookouts across what we hope will be the line of return march of the Comanche raiding party."

"Then as soon as they see anything we respond in force?"

"Almost. I sat in on the planning session with the two colonels and Major Stanton. The lookouts will be about half a mile apart and equipped with mirrors to flash one another. They will flash on the hour starting at the farthest one and working to the last one on this end. They've worked out some kind of code.''

"Like they use on the telegraph?" Delaney asked.

"I don't know. Here's the important part. The colonel expects the hostiles to be gone from here for four days. On day four he wants to have in place along that line about two hundred men. The next day he'll send out another two hundred. That way there won't be a big dust trail to warn the Comanches. We hope to get a line on their trail and ambush them.''

"Ambush a Comanche, I'll bet," Philburton said. "I wish us well.''

"The least we can do is bend in the end of our lines and surround them," Westcott said. "Then we'll see what kind of fighters they are.''

"But how does our man get close enough to the colonel with maybe four hundred troops out there?" Delaney asked.

"That's why this might not be the time for the shoot. But if it works out, we'll be ready." Westcott frowned. "Oh, we haven't collected yet. Since Hartsook isn't with us, the ante went up. He's demanding two hundred dollars, sixty-six dollars each.''

"Getting damn expensive.''

"Depends on what we get for our cash," Westcott replied. "If it doesn't happen, we get the money back. I'll hold on to it.''

"Good thing we got paid last week," Delaney said.

Captain Philburton got up and stretched. "Damn, we have anything else to talk about? I got to get home and do the old woman once to keep her happy.''

"Right, it's getting late. Keep your man up to date on what's happening. Like I said, we don't need to know who he is.''

Philburton nodded and left by the back door in the darkness.

Major Westcott waited until he heard the back door

to his bachelor quarters close, then motioned to Delaney. "You said you could stand making a few extra dollars, right?"

"Yeah, right now I'm not too particular how I do it."

"Good. I want to talk to you about a slick retail proposition we have working. No, more like a whole-sale operation. Hartsook was helping, but now he's gone. Let me fill you in on what we do, how we do it, and what I'll expect of you for your fifty percent of the profits."

The next morning Canyon O'Grady and Captain Lancer went to the quarters of the late Lieutenant Hartsook. There would be an official inventory of his gear, army equipment returned to the quartermaster, his personal items boxed up and shipped to his listed next-of-kin. That would come later in the day.

The two officers worked through the bachelor quarters for an hour. They didn't know exactly what they were looking for. Canyon found something interesting in the back of a dresser drawer filled with mementos, old magazines, and various other discards and trash. Inside a leather pouch with a drawstring, he found seven gold double eagles and a goodly portion of gold dust dotted with small nuggets the size of buckshot.

"Well, well," Canyon said, showing the find to Lancer. "How do you suppose that Lieutenant Hartsook came up with a small fortune like this?"

"Interesting," Captain Lancer said. "Now where in the hell would he get just-panned gold dust and small bits of free gold?"

"Maybe from some Comanchero who traded rifles to some Cheyenne warriors up in Colorado?"

"Damn, we were so close to him."

"You find out anything about his buddies, who he got drunk with?"

"Not a whisper, Colonel. All we've got is the poker game, and that's not enough to hang anybody."

"Might be. Gold has a special footprint. Take it to a chemical analyst and he can tell you where the gold came from. In this case, if they split the gold dust, we could prove that what we have here came from the same bag that somebody else had."

"The problem is we don't have a chemical laboratory here to do the analysis."

"Right, but whoever has the other half of that gold wouldn't know that. We might be able to spook somebody into saying something or doing something."

"Oh, ran into another interesting item. Five troopers in two companies reportedly lost their rifles during campaigns against the Indians, and only reported the fact a few days ago."

"Strange. Doesn't anybody check closer than that on personal weapons?"

"Not these two outfits. In my company, I'd know it at least within a day."

"So maybe these men didn't lose them, but sold them to a certain officer who needed five more for his delivery to the Comanchero."

"Possible. But if it holds, probably the same officer did the buying who grabbed the surveyed rifles. The same one who will be buried tomorrow."

"Still, nose it around, see what you can find out. Maybe have one of your trusted enlisted men do the job. They'd get the ear of the five men quicker."

"That will be the easy part. If Colonel Colton is putting four hundred men out in the field along that line within four days, how can we have any chance of getting the killer who our pair of unknown plotters might send out there? Even if we know of the worst men in the regiment, we can't restrict them all to the base, not all thirty-six of them."

"Yes, a problem, I'm working on it. I have an idea

113

that just might work. If that band of Comanches does come back the same way it left . . .''

"They usually go the shortest route on these long trips. Sometimes they travel five or six hundred miles on a raid. They are probably the best horsemen I've ever seen."

Canyon nodded. "If they come back this general direction, some of our men should spot them early enough. Now, I'll let you get back to your company. I'm writing out a receipt for this cash and gold dust. I want you to sign it and I'll sign it stating where we found it. Then you turn it over to the colonel and pull the guard off here and watch it and see who comes to take a look inside. If Hartsook has a partner, he'll know about the gold, if it came from the sale of the rifles. He might try to get it back."

"That would be his coconspirator on the rifles?"

"Could be. This place has no back door. The windows are locked. I'll take the first four hours, and then you come and relieve me. It's a little after ten in the morning. I'll see you about two."

"Where will you be?"

"Somewhere that will let me see the front door, but that won't let anyone trying the latch see me. Oh, let's leave it unlocked, and the special guard is on only at night."

"You are sneaky," Captain Lancer said, grinning.

"That's why I'm a colonel."

Captain Lancer took the leather pouch of gold and coins to give it to the colonel, and Canyon found a spot three houses along that had a porch. A bush grew beside the porch and Canyon could see the Hartsook quarters from there yet remain out of sight behind the shrub.

He knocked and a sprightly woman in her thirties came to the door. He introduced himself and explained he needed to watch down the street for a while without being obvious.

"Would it be all right if I used your outside rocking chair over there on the front porch?"

"Well, of course, Colonel O'Grady. Good to see you again. We danced once at the colonel's the other night."

"Yes, that was a fine party. Now I'll just sit down and not be a bother."

Canyon sat there for two hours and no one even slowed down going past the target. The lady of the house, who introduced herself as Lieutenant Tucker Vallis' wife, Virginia, brought him out a sandwich and a glass of lemonade.

Just after noon an officer walked toward the quarters, looked around, and tried the door. He seemed to hesitate a moment, then went inside quickly. Canyon was too far away to identify the man. An officer, but which one out of the twenty-four on post? Canyon gave him fifteen minutes, which should be plenty of time for a search. Then Canyon strolled in that direction. He walked past the spot and fifty yards into the quad, then reversed his direction.

He went three houses down the other way along the walk and stopped. Canyon knew he would become obvious if he kept up the pacing. He decided to go back to the Vallis house and wait. When the man came out, he would try to overtake him.

Canyon was just a few steps from the Hartsook quarters when the door opened and a man came out whom Canyon didn't know. He was one of the few that Canyon hadn't had a private talk with yet.

With a big smile Colonel O'Grady held out his hand. "Yes, Captain, I've been hoping I'd run into you. Haven't had our little chat yet, and now would be a fine time for me. Do you have anything that can't be postponed for fifteen minutes?"

The man looked startled, then seemed to relax and caught the colonel's hand and shook it.

"No, sir. Where should we talk?"

"These your quarters? Perhaps in there."

"No, sir, not mine, just . . . just visiting a friend. I'm down about six units. Be glad to have you there."

They talked for twenty minutes. Canyon found out the man's name was Captain Erin Delaney, and he was commanding officer of C Company. The name was really all he wanted. He left the man, telling him to keep up the good work, and walked leisurely toward the Regimental GHQ.

Colonel Colton met Canyon as soon as he came in, and waved him into his private office. When the door was closed, Colonel Colton dropped the leather bag on his desk.

"What the hell is this about gold dust?"

"Good question. Near as I can tell there simply isn't any free gold in any of the streams around here. That's high-mountain-grade color."

"So what the hell is it doing in Lieutenant Hartsook's dresser?"

"I was hoping you could help me on that, Colonel."

"I don't have the whit of an idea."

"I have a guess. Last month your command surveyed thirteen army rifles for breakdown. Only two of them were actually ready for survey and they were broken into spare parts. An officer threatened the armorer and made him sign the forms showing the breakdown of the other eleven.

"The officer who did that bit of dirty work was Lieutenant Ira Hartsook. The armorer confessed when he heard that the officer had been lost on that patrol. I put an armed guard on the dead man's door and this morning Captain Lancer and I found the gold.

"We think Hartsook and someone else of higher

116

rank have set up a contact to deliver rifles to a Comanchero, who pays for them in gold and sells the rifles in Colorado, where he gets gold for them that the Indians steal from the whites up there."

Colonel Colton sat down, nodding. "Makes sense. Too bad he didn't live through that attack. I would have enjoyed hanging him. But then, maybe he got killed with one of the rifles he sold to the Indians."

"It would be a fond hope, Colonel, but I doubt if he would take that chance. A vow by the Comanchero to sell them far away would undoubtedly be asked."

"Who is the other man involved?"

"Colonel, I don't know. I have a suspect, but no evidence. I'm working on it. How are the preparations for the blockade line going?"

"According to plan. We have out six six-man patrols scattered on a line due west of the fort for twenty miles. Each with a mirror. Tomorrow we send out another twelve teams of six men to fill in the spaces between the first group. That means we'll have a lookout group of six men each mile from here and out twenty miles."

"The fourth day you figure the Comanches will be back. Where will you concentrate your troops?"

"I'll put one company of sixty men on the spot where the Comanche trail heads south. Then I'll position two companies on each side of the center line at a distance of a half-mile each.

"That means I can concentrate three hundred men anywhere within that two-mile area quickly. The units have all been instructed to take cover in draws or gullies or behind small rises. Anywhere that they can hide from the heathen until the last moment."

"Sounds like a fine plan, Colonel. Oh, that gold. I want you to hold it as evidence for me. If you're getting ready to send the lieutenant's personal gear to his next-of-kin, I want the gold kept out of it."

"Good. Ill-gotten gains and all that."

"Oh, Colonel. You remember what I talked about before concerning your continuing good health?"

"Yes."

"Will you be riding on the fourth day with the five companies of troops?"

"Absolutely! I want to avenge the deaths of those seven troopers. Couldn't keep me away with a undertaker's black hearse."

"Colonel, I hope that isn't a slip of the tongue that is a harbinger of what's to come. I'm asking you again to stay here and let your field commanders handle the action. They are entirely qualified."

"Hell, no. It's my duty to be there. Until you take it away from me, this is my post and I'm in charge."

"True, Colonel, entirely true. I just hope that you'll live through the next week and won't have to regret this decision. Now, it seems I've missed my dinner. If you'll excuse me."

Canyon's orderly-cook had made a soup for dinner and it was bubbling on the back of the wood-fired stove. The sandwich from Mrs. Vallis had just sharpened his appetite. The soup was good. After the food, Canyon stopped by at Captain Lancer's quarters. He was still there.

"Spotted him," Canyon said. "Only one man came around looking for something in Hartsook's quarters, probably the gold. He didn't find it. He was Captain Erin Delaney."

"Delaney? He's one of the four who play poker every week. I found out who the other two were, Lieutenant Hartsook we knew and Captain Lewis Philburton. Those three and Major Westcott were the quartet."

"Delaney could be in on the plot for the rifle sales. All we have to do is watch the three of them."

"How, with only two of us?"

"You have an orderly and so do I, that makes four. I can get two more men assigned and we'll watch them from now on all night. If they move, we've got them."

"What about the colonel? Will he be going out on the fourth day?"

"Bet on it."

"That's going to be big trouble."

"You can count on it."

"I'd rather not."

"Then help me come up with a way to keep him on the post short of tying him to his chair."

12

Captain Lancer and Canyon talked for two hours about the problem of how to keep the colonel at the fort but came up with nothing that would work.

The captain asked Canyon to stay for supper and he sent word to his orderly he would be out.

At last Canyon had a glimmer of an idea.

"We can't keep the colonel on the post without ruining his career. My job here is partly to preserve that career. He'll be needed in administration in the big war that probably is coming.

"We can't restrict to post all thirty-six of those malcontents who could include a sniper set to kill the colonel. But what we can do is pick out the four worst of the lot, the four who are capable of murder for hire, and stick so close to them that they won't have a chance to fire at the colonel, or if they do, we'll have an eyewitness to the deed."

"Not good odds, Colonel. The chances are nine-to-one that we miss the man."

"Not when we figure in the records and reputations of these worst types. I'd say our chances are more like fifty-fifty. Let's look at that list of bad apples you had from the companies."

They worked over the list for another hour, and at last came up with the worst four. Two of them were from Fox Company, one each from Able and How companies. They examined the records of the four troublemakers, and ranked the two in Fox as number one and number three, the number-two worst man was from Able and the last from How Company.

"I've got to stay with the colonel on the march," Canyon said. "Why don't you shadow F Company and cover the two men. I'll have my orderly, Sergeant O'Hallohan, stay with A Company, and we'll use one of our special men from the shadowing detail on the poker players to watch over the bad ass in How."

"Colonel, we might have a glimmer of a chance now. We might."

"One flaw. What happens if Fox and Able aren't on the hike that day? Or if these malcontents get sent out as lookouts. They might already be out there."

"I'll check with the adjutant, right now, and be back."

"Before you go, one more item. If the killer's unit isn't assigned, I'd bet that he is put into some other unit to tag along. He might have enough rating to make that possible. If we can find such a man out of his unit, we've probably spotted the killer."

"That would be a lucky break. I'll get over to GHQ and check to see if any of our thirty-six men are already out on the twenty-mile line, and also try to find out who is set to go out on the fourth day."

"Don't be long, Daddy," Cindy Lance said from the door to the kitchen. "Supper will be ready soon."

"I'll be back. Come in here and talk to Colonel O'Grady until I get back."

"Golly, that's a pretty tough assignment, Daddy." She giggled. "But I'll try to be pleasant."

Captain Lancer waved and hurried out the front door.

Cindy sat on the couch three feet from Canyon and at once he felt his desire for the girl surging. She was the same slightly sassy and saucy wench, with her long dark hair and oval face that left him wishing they were in his quarters and alone. He kept visualizing her naked on his bed the way they both had been a few nights ago, panting and moaning and making love furiously.

"That's a strange look you have, Canyon," she said softly.

Her mother was busy in the kitchen cooking and singing a song softly that was a half-note off-key.

"Unbridled passion is what you saw," Canyon half-whispered.

She grinned and moved closer to him. The curious smile turned lustful.

"I wish there was something I could do about your hardness problem right here and right now," she whispered. "But Mother is just out in the kitchen."

Cindy's back was to that door. He moved closer and reached out and rubbed her surging breasts.

She caught his hand and pressed it there hard for a moment, then moved it away. "You do that again, Colonel, and I'll explode," Cindy whispered. She shifted slightly away from him. "Colonel," she said brightly in her normal voice, "we can practice playing bridge and learn more of the rules."

"It seems there are thousands of rules."

"So we should play more so we can learn them all. Then we can play with my parents tonight. Let's go over the basic rules again. There's a deck of cards here somewhere."

They talked about the rules again and Canyon laid out sample hands and played all four.

Soon Captain Lancer was back and they had supper. He brought good news. Only two of the men on the "list of thirty-six" were on the picket line. Both of them were low-risk types.

"Fox and Able are both set to go on the attack group on the fourth day, so our top three suspects are covered."

That evening they played bridge. Captain Lancer and Cindy caught on to it quickly, but it was a struggle again for Mrs. Lancer. Canyon never had a chance to touch the girl until she shook his hand good night.

The next two days, they had their surveillance of the three officers in full operation. Their quarters were watched from six P.M. to four A.M. every day. None of the three made any special trips or did anything out of the ordinary.

"We'll have them keep up the watch even when we're gone on the raid," Canyon said. "Captain Delaney is commanding officer of Able Company and Philburton of Fox, so both of them will be on the operation. Still we'll have the men tail the major."

The fatal fourth day after they found the Comanche trail heading south, they filed out from the fort. They left at three A.M. and rode at a steady pace of four miles an hour through the night.

This was the major troop movement to entrap the Comanche.

"We'll ride at night so there won't be a trace of a dust cloud left in the air by daylight," Colonel Colton told Canyon. "That way we'll have plenty of time to find our places of concealment long before even an advance scout could be in this area."

As they left the main gate, they made quite a parade with five companies of men, a few over three hundred, on the march. They were in good spirits, and this was a change in the dull routine of the army post. Anything different was welcome even if it involved a chance that they might soon be facing the deadly Comanche warriors.

At the ambush areas, the two colonels rode from one company to the next, helping to place the men out of sight in gullies and behind the few low rises that were in this part of the east Texas countryside.

One company was on the line twelve miles from the post. Another was a mile beyond that and A Company and the colonel a mile farther at the site of the old Comanche trail. Two more companies were hidden a mile each on to the west. The only change in the plan was that they had moved the main body to the line of the tracks of the Comanches where they went south. That was about fourteen miles from the post. They had lookouts five miles back toward Fort Johnson and more out fifteen miles beyond the old trail.

"I figure the heathens won't come closer than fourteen or fifteen miles to the fort, so we'll concentrate here but stretch our picket line out fifteen miles the other way," Colonel Colton said. "We'll keep mobile so we can move to concentrate in one area when we get a direction they're coming toward us."

He stared south with hatred in his eyes. "If all else fails and we don't get to ambush the bastards, we'll give chase. Their horses will be tired by this time. Ours will be fresh in another two or three hours."

Back at the fort, Canyon had thought he might be able to lead the colonel out of the action, get lost with him somehow. But now he saw that wouldn't work. There were always five men in the detail that escorted the colonel from one company position to the other. He couldn't take all of them into his confidence, and neither could he trick them into getting lost. If there was a fight, there would be little he could do to protect the colonel.

They waited.

Canyon, the colonel, and his entourage had returned to A Company, which was less than one hundred yards from the Comanche's south trail. They were concealed in two slight gullies not more than ten feet deep and had forward lookouts on foot a quarter of a mile in front of them looking south. The other companies were concealed by an hour after daylight and had lookouts in position.

Canyon had talked to Captain Lancer, who had asked to be assigned to F Company. He had identified the two malcontents who were number one and number three on the killer list. Lancer knew who they were and would watch them if there was a firefight.

Canyon asked about the man in Able Company. His name was Kell Jefferson. It wasn't Irish for Kelly, rather of Norse origin. Sergeant O'Hallohan had talked with him. He was a sergeant as well and was a favorite of Captain Delaney, who was CO of the company.

Sergeant O'Hallohan said he'd be right beside the man if there was a firefight.

Still they waited.

Noon came and went and the men had a cold meal from their rations. Some chewed on the ever-present hardtack. The salt pork was impossible to eat without cooking. A few soaked the hardtack in their big cooking cups in cold water and ate it that way.

For one day they wouldn't starve to death.

It was nearly three that afternoon when the advance scout came running back to Able Company. He had spotted a good-sized dust trail coming at a slight angle to him. He figured they would meet the line about a mile to the west.

The lookout was sent back out a half-mile to estimate the distance of the dust and direction again. He was back in an hour this time on his horse.

"Sir, estimate the dust trail is six to eight miles away. They are definitely angled to the west of our position. I'd say they will hit our line about five miles west."

Colonel Colton had sent out One Hand Ready with the trooper. One Hand Ready shook his head. "Two miles west of us," he said.

Colonel Colton frowned and dismissed both men,

sending them back to the same position. The Colonel quickly gave orders for messengers to go bring the two companies on the east side and move them to a position five miles west of Able Company and three miles from the farthest-positioned company.

"Tell the officer commanding that the men should move in concealment if possible, and to move slowly in single file to help hold down any dust."

An hour later the two companies moved past Able Company's position, working small draws and gullies and the few low hills.

The two colonels rode south to the Able Company outpost and looked at the dust. It was coming this way. There was little wind today and the dust hung in the sky, rose a little, and slowly dissipated.

"Maybe three miles to the west," Colonel Colton said.

"To the west for sure," Canyon agreed. "I couldn't tell you how far." They watched the dust cloud moving again. The riders were probably still five miles away.

"I hear these raiders travel fast, seven or eight miles an hour," Canyon went on. "How do they do it?"

"Those desert ponies they breed. Sturdy, hardy, small. Can run all day at eight miles an hour, I bet. Damn hard in a chase against our heavier grain-fed horses."

They rode back to the line. The second company had come past.

"We have a gap in the middle of our line now," Colonel Colton said. "I'm thinking of moving A Company there."

Canyon frowned. "I'm wondering if the Comanches won't turn this way. They are creatures of habit. They came this way before from a long way north. Why not use the same trail, one that they know?"

"Not a chance. We're going to box them in," Colonel Colton said. He looked where the dust could now be seen from the blocking line, frowned, then shook his head. "No, we've got the right deployment. I'm moving up that way." He stopped. "No, think I'll stay here and wait for some better indication of their direction. We've got at least an hour, maybe more before the heathens will be here."

Canyon nodded and rode into the small gully where the men of Able Company were sitting around waiting. Some of them rested in the shade of their mounts. There were two games of pitch going and some poker.

Canyon ignored Sergeant O'Hallohan as they had agreed to do. The sergeant was three men away from Kell Jefferson, their number-two candidate for the sniper. So far Canyon had been able to keep Colonel Colton behind his lines except for the one ride to the outpost.

So far, so good.

An hour later, Canyon sat with Colonel Colton in a draw among the men of Able Company. All were mounted now. The hostiles had altered their direction to come more toward the center of the line of five companies.

Then, as they watched, the band turned sharply to the left, bearing directly at A Company where it was isolated on the end of the far-strung-out five-company line.

Drastic action was needed. A runner should be sent toward the next company—H or F, he forgot which—ordering it to move toward A Company at once.

It was too early for a bugle call; that would alert the savages.

Canyon O'Grady looked at Colonel Colton for his orders. Action was needed at once.

Canyon saw the colonel's face working; his eyes went wide as he stared at the oncoming Comanche

127

now less than a quarter of a mile away and headed straight for A Company along the old trail.

Colonel Colton looked at the men around him, started to say something. He drew his saber half out of its scabbard, then frowned and slid it back.

"Colonel, we have to make some adjustments on the line," Canyon said quietly to the man stirrup to stirrup beside him.

Colonel Colton turned toward him, smiling. There was a vagueness about his eyes, and now he grinned. "Hell, Colonel, polo isn't what it used to be. Even here in Washington it's too damn civilized a sport."

The colonel was out of the battle.

Canyon whirled and pointed at a corporal. "Trooper, take the colonel's reins and lead him to the rear down this gully at once. Go at least a half-mile and wait for orders. Do it now, corporal!"

The trooper jumped his mount forward, took the reins out of the colonel's hands, and got only a smile in return. Then the trooper led the colonel down the gully away from the action.

The savages were within two hundred yards of the troops. They had slowed and now Canyon looked for the bugler. He was always supposed to be near the commander. He spotted him.

"Bugler, sound the charge, repeat it four times."

Canyon took out his six-gun and readied the big bronze stallion for the charge forward. This was no sleeping village. This was a fight for his life. The bugler blew the notes.

"Charge," Colonel Canyon O'Grady bellowed, and the members of A Company, Fourth Cavalry Regiment, surged forward over the top of the gully and slammed forward toward the forty Comanche warriors, who saw that it was too late to turn and run.

13

Canyon O'Grady charged forward with Able Company troopers on both sides of him. Some fired their carbines, some had out revolvers. The company had been set up in a gentle arc so they came at the surprised Comanches from in front and about thirty degrees on each side, leaving only one exit, to the rear.

Two of the warriors went down on the first volley of rifle fire from a hundred yards. The second gush of fire from the long guns downed four of the Indian ponies and three more warriors were blasted from their ponies.

A moment later the two forces had closed, and it was pistols against a few lances, short knives and war axes.

One warrior lifted high on his pony's back to swing his war ax with a metal blade. It half-severed a trooper's left arm, but before the trooper fell off his mount, he brought his revolver around and fired into the warrior's grinning face from two feet away, blowing one eye into gristle and mush and jolting the top of his skull off.

The troopers fired carefully at times, then wildly. Each man knew he had six shots before reloading, and with cap and ball it took considerable time. Most men made the six shots count.

Two troopers fell early to arrows, but the blue-shirts were upon the Comanches before they could use their bows to good effect.

Six warriors faded to the rear, then lit out for the south. One sergeant ordered ten of his men to chase the warriors. They fired their single-shot rifles and brought down two, then gained on the weary Indian ponies, shot two more savages off the animals, and chased down the final two warriors, killing them with a flurry of rifle fire.

The main battle moved back and forth on the high plains. Four Comanche riders broke through the ring of blue-shirts and rode like demons for the north not looking back, crouched low over their ponies as they went.

A herd of about two hundred stolen horses that young Indian boys drove some quarter-mile to the rear were abandoned when the young men saw their warriors in trouble. The youth fled in both east and west directions to circle around the trouble spot.

Canyon knocked down a warrior with his first revolver shot, then disabled two more who hit the ground running into a narrow gully where a horse couldn't follow. He whirled around, dodged a lance a warrior aimed for him as he kicked his war pony forward.

O'Grady dropped to the far side of his mount, Indian-style, to avoid the lance, then shot the warrior as the Comanche spun his mount and tried with the lance again.

When Canyon whirled his mount to check behind him, he found only six warriors still fighting. They had been trapped on the ground and fell to revolver rounds within seconds. Another half a dozen Comanches kicked their tough little Indian mounts to the east, rounding the last of the blue-shirts and streaking to the north.

The colonel! Canyon saw that Captain Delaney had control of his forces and was assembling them, checking the wounded Comanche and dispatching those that required it. The Fourth had never taken an Indian captive and never would, the men bragged.

Canyon turned and spurred Cormac to the rear into the gully they had hidden in, and followed it north, where it grew slightly wider.

About a hundred yards from the battle scene, he found three horses, and slightly farther on he saw Colonel Colton sitting beside the bank whittling with a penknife.

The corporal who had led the colonel away from the battle lay nearby with a bloody wound on the side of his head. He wasn't moving.

Riding up on the top of the bank came Sergeant O'Hallohan. He pushed a man ahead of him. The trooper had his hands tied to the saddle and O'Hallohan kept his revolver trained on the man.

"We've got him," O'Hallohan called to O'Grady.

"I got here just a little late. This skunk left the main battle and raced this way, jumped off his horse, and went down in a prone position. Before I could get here, he fired his carbine. Then I put a .44 slug through his shoulder and he caved in. He's the one we've been hunting, all right."

Canyon took a closer look at the trooper. He was Sergeant Kell Jefferson. "You're sure, Sergeant?"

"Absolutely. I saw him fire the round that killed the corporal. Jefferson simply missed his target. He never was good with a rifle. Everyone knows that."

Canyon rode to where Colonel Colton sat whittling. He stepped down and squatted beside the bird colonel. Colton's eyes were still vague, simple, uninvolved.

"Colonel, isn't it about time we find your horse?" Canyon asked.

"Hell, man, I broke my polo mallet. Just had the one. No sense me even riding today."

Canyon slapped the colonel sharply on the cheek. The officer's eyes went wide for a moment. He stared at Canyon and his face started to get red, then he closed his eyes and shook his head. When he opened his eyes, they were clear and sharp.

"What the hell am I doing unhorsed?" he asked,

his voice between a snap and a snarl. "Have the damn Comanche come yet? What the hell is happening?"

Canyon pointed to the dead man beside him.

"God! Is he hurt bad? Call the doctor."

"Too late," Canyon said.

"Where's my horse?"

"Back there about fifty yards, Colonel."

"The damn Comanche turn and ride away? Where is the battle? What's happening?"

"The battle is over, Colonel Colton. Remember I told you that you blocked out everything twice before. You wouldn't believe me. It happened again. When things don't go right, or when there is some intense emotional problem, you simply turn off your mind, you block everything out and live in a dream world of some pleasant memory."

"You're telling me I'm crazy?" Colonel Colton said, his face a mask of surprise, anger, and dejection.

"Not at all. What I'm telling you is that you don't have many options left. You must either ask for a transfer from this post, or stop going on combat patrols, or answer the second letter I have for you from the president."

Colton sat there staring at his hands. Then he looked at the dead man beside him. "This dead boy, how did that happen?"

"Remember I told you I'd heard of a death threat against you? They tried; they hired a trooper to kill you. He got excited and worried that he was followed and he shot too quickly and missed you, but hit the corporal. We'll find out who hired him and send them to prison for murder."

"This corporal's death is my fault."

"No, no death of a soldier is ever the commander's fault. It's part of the system. Now, let's get you back on your horse. The battle is over. I saw the other companies coming this way. We should be ready to march back to the fort in an hour or so. I want you to lead us back the same way you led us out here. Nobody expects the colonel to be in the middle of a big fight.''

Back at the battle scene, Able Company was pulling itself together. They had suffered eight dead, but counted twenty-nine Comanche warrior dead. There would be much wailing in the raider's camp.

"Leave them where they fell," Colonel Colton ordered. "They will be back to claim their dead. Let them. Take bows and arrows and war axes if you wish. All weapons left here are to be destroyed and the metal arrowheads and ax heads and lance points will be taken to the fort with us and melted down.''

There were twenty-one wounded. The fort physician was hard at work on four of them. It was determined that they could not travel. Fox Company was ordered to stay behind as a rear guard for the doctor and his patients. One of the four died before the main body left.

Twenty men who said they had some cowboy experience were detailed to go down and round up the stolen horses and drive them back to the fort. There was a chance some of them could be used for remounts, and the others given to ranchers or offered for sale. It was a new problem that hadn't come up before. The animals were too good to be destroyed.

Able Company's dead were tied over their saddles, the wounded who could ride were lifted onto their mounts, and the rest of the troops left for the fort.

It would be a fourteen-mile ride of pain for many of them.

On the way back, Colonel Colton and Canyon O'Grady led the troops. They had out a ten-man point a half-mile ahead and ten security details along each side of the lead units.

Colonel Colton looked over at Canyon and frowned.

"Back there you said that you had a second letter for me from the president?''

"Yes, sir, that's correct."

"What does it say?"

"I don't know. Not my business. It's sealed and to be given to you only when I determined that your other options are limited."

"Such as my staying in the fort or asking for a transfer?"

"Yes, sir."

They rode along in silence for a ways.

"O'Grady, I want to thank you. That's twice now you saved my butt. If I'd been left up there at the battle site, some Comanche would have made me look like an arrow pincushion."

"A chance of that, yes, sir. For your information, I think you're right, about a big war coming. There will be a big need for top brass. You earned your eagles without being in the pressure of combat. No sense in saying you can't get a star or two without any more dodging bullets. You've earned your spurs, sir. I'm sure the president will agree."

"Yes, but I know that James Buchanan is not going to run for reelection."

"You didn't use your White House contacts to get your eagles. You won't need it for your star."

When the troops arrived at the fort, the rest of the soldiers and most of the women came out to greet them. One of the dead troopers was married. His wife blinked back the tears and strode along beside her husband's horse, which carried his body.

Canyon saw that Sergeant Jefferson was put directly into the disciplinary barracks cell attached to the guardhouse. O'Grady had a good meal and then went with Colonel Colton to question the man.

They worked on him for two hours and found that they knew absolutely nothing more than they did when they started. They knew his name and rank and unit, and that was it.

He kept screaming that Sergeant O'Hallohan hated him and made up the whole thing. Nobody saw it happen, but O'Hallohan and a court-martial would have one man's story against another's. No court would ever convict on that.

Jefferson screamed at them and they screamed back at him. The two officers left and a half-hour later, Jefferson was released. Canyon watched him come out of the disciplinary barracks.

"Jefferson, just a gentle suggestion. You don't have to take the punishment for this alone. If you don't tell us who paid you to do this, we'll find out and then you'll be hung. Oh, if you're thinking of riding away, don't. There'll be triple guards on every horse and stable area tonight. If you want to run, you'll have to do it on your own two feet. Just a word of warning."

It was dark by then. Jefferson snorted and hurried away. As he did, four specially briefed men faded into the shadows and followed Jefferson.

Canyon nodded. He would know everything that Jefferson did. The four men would establish a box around him and record everyone he talked to and looked at, everywhere he went, and everything he did. Sooner or later he'd make a mistake.

O'Grady went to see the fort commander. He stopped by his quarters and took out the envelope, which was carefully wrapped in waxed paper inside a larger envelope.

The colonel had just finished his nightly reading and leaned back in his comfortable chair in the living room.

"Colonel O'Grady. About this afternoon. I mean, is there any need to . . . to tell anyone else?" He looked at the kitchen, where his wife was noisily putting away a lot of pots and pans.

Canyon shook his head. "Only the man you got the letter from in Washington. No one else."

"Good. I don't want that other envelope. Not yet. There are two problems left for us to solve. Who that man today with the rifle was hired by, and who is behind the rifles being sold to the Indians. I won't leave this place with two unsolved matters like those."

Canyon told Colton what he was doing on both counts. He told the colonel about the four men shadowing Jefferson.

"Sooner or later he'll have to go talk to the ones who hired him, and then we'll have the whole conspiracy. Right now we don't have any idea. It could be one man, perhaps two or three. Our betting is that it's an officer. Which leaves me with twenty-one suspects. That leaves out you and Captain Lancer from the twenty-three officers now in the regiment."

"Ummmmm. I have no idea who it might be. What about the rifles?"

"There we have something to work with. Lieutenant Hartsook was one of them. He forced the altered files to get the ten rifles. He might also have been the man who bought the last five rifles from the enlisted men.

"From there we're concentrating on the men he played poker with. Major Westcott, Captain Delaney, and Captain Philburton. So far we have no evidence, but we have had around-the-clock watches on all three men for three days now. It'll go back on tonight. All we can do now is wait."

"Looks like you're doing a good job. You going to tell me what you really do besides pretend to be a U.S. army colonel?"

"Not yet, Colonel."

"When we get these other two problems taken care of, then we'll look at that second letter and decide just what to do."

"Sounds good, Colonel. I better get back to work."

14

The two officers stood in the dark behind the stables. "Sure, Delaney, you're tired," Major Westcott said. "All you did was go on a thirty-mile joyride. So you had a little scuffle with a few Comanche today. That's done. Tonight the two of us stand to make some money, and you damn well are going along."

"Look, I'm so tired I couldn't even ride a horse. How far is this meeting?"

"Hell, that's the beauty of it. We only ride out two miles to a little stream and a big cottonwood. You can ride two miles in your sleep. I've already got the horses stashed out there in a gully and the goods are in my quarters. We wait until midnight and take a ride."

"Goddamn! You'll have to wake me up before we go and when we get there. How many rifles?"

"Ten, all I could get," Westcott said softly. "I stole a few, bought a few, but the sods who sold them didn't see my face and can't identify me. Done in the dark when you were out playing soldier."

"Christ, you talk like a crazy man." Delaney held up his hands. "Okay, okay, I'll go. Let me get three hours of sleep first. That always used to be enough for me."

"It's eight o'clock now," Major Westcott said. "Be at my place at midnight, or I simply get a new partner."

"I'll be there. Now let me get some sleep." He

walked off through the barns and sheds and out the far end before he headed for officers' row on the far side of the parade grounds.

Major Westcott went out the front doors of the stable as if he belonged there, and marched straight across the parade grounds to his quarters.

Ten minutes later Canyon listened to the corporal who had been watching the two officers along with the three other men. Both officers were still under scrutiny, but evidently inside their quarters for the night.

"You say they went by devious routes and then met behind the stables and talked?"

"Yes, sir. Quite a heated conversation. I heard Captain Delaney flare up once and say he was too tired to go out tonight."

"Good, go tell Captain Lancer I need to see him right away, and tell him to come prepared to take a ride."

Just after midnight, Captain Lancer and Canyon trailed the two officers away from Major Westcott's quarters.

"I think we hit pay dirt," Canyon said.

"Where do you think they're headed?"

"Can't tell. They're both walking, and both are carrying what looks like to be heavy wrapped packages. Long packages."

"The kind that could hold rifles?" Captain Lancer asked.

"The very same."

Canyon and the captain had taken out their horses past the double guards an hour earlier to be ready. The guards reported that no other horses had been checked in or out since dark.

"They going to walk all the way?" Captain Lancer asked.

"If it were me, I'd have a pair of horses hidden down on one of these little brushy creeks. We'll see."

138

"I can't believe those two carrying loads that heavy very far," Lancer said.

Five minutes later, Canyon and Lancer crouched near some brush and watched the two officers tie the bundles on back of their saddles and ride nearly due west from the fort. The watchers followed at a safe distance, so they were able to make them out in the cloudless night that boasted a half moon.

Twice they lost the pair ahead. They had to ride faster and swept out at angles to make sure the targets hadn't turned. Each time they found the pair walking their mounts forward, still due west.

It took only a half-hour for the gun-runners to come to a stop. It was beside a big cottonwood on the edge of a small stream that was nearly dry. It had been a dry summer in Texas.

Canyon and Lancer moved their horses back a hundred yards, then crept up slowly on foot. By the time they got where they could see plainly again, there was a third man talking with the pair. He didn't wear a uniform. No other horse was visible. The new man had come in from the other way and must have left his horse out there, Canyon decided.

Cautiously Canyon and Lancer worked closer until they could hear the talk. Both carried the new seven-shot Spencer repeating carbines with two extra tubes tied to the stock.

"Don't give a damn what I paid for the other ones, these are worth no more than thirty-five dollars each to me. Take it or leave it."

"Where else you gonna get rifles that good?" Captain Delaney asked. "It's a good deal."

"Might be, but I'm running out of gold. I'll have to do some high trading to come out ahead even at thirty-five a rifle."

"Not when you stole the gold from them Cheyenne up in Colorado," Major Westcott said with a laugh.

"Hell, Long Jack, we know how you got the gold. Cheap come, cheap go, I always say. We'll take the thirty-five each. Now, how about an order for some army short knives and bayonets and sabers?"

"I can't give away the sabers. But those knives are interesting. Take about twenty-five each of the knives and bayonets. You get me that many?"

"Easy, in two weeks."

"I'll be here. Worth a dollar a blade."

"Five dollars each," Westcott bargained.

A few minutes later they reached a price of three dollars each and shook hands.

"Now for the rifles," Westcott said. He untied the bundle from his horse and lifted it down.

Canyon touched Lancer and they pulled back twenty yards.

"He must have somebody else behind that brush. I'll swing around there and you witness the rifle sale. When I fire the first shot, shoot somebody in the legs and we close in."

It took Canyon ten minutes of slow going to circle the spot and come in from behind. He found two horses, one with a pack rig, but no other man. He untied the horses and moved them down the stream and hid them fifty yards behind the brush.

Then he moved gently back toward the big cottonwood tree. He got there in time to see the money change hands and the two officers turn toward their horses.

"Far enough! Hands in the air," Long Jack barked. "Don't even turn around, this six-gun has all chambers loaded, that's three slugs for each of you before you can spit."

"What the hell you doing, Long Jack?" Westcott roared, but he didn't turn.

"Do? I'm getting my three hundred and fifty dollars back. I should have done this the last time, but I figured you had a rifle in the brush out there somewhere. Tonight you don't."

Canyon moved slightly for a better shot past some brush. He sighted in on the Comanchero's right shoulder. That would knock down the weapon. Canyon squeezed the trigger gently and fired.

The round ripped through Long Jack's shoulder, but was a little high, not knocking down the gun. He bellowed in pain and spun around, but he had no target.

Westcott and Delaney charged away from the man going at angles to each other and both pawing for their own six-guns on their hips. The major surged behind his horse and whirled to fire under the mount's neck.

Long Jack had vanished. The ten rifles lay on the ground where they had just been inspected.

"Where the hell is he?" Westcott roared.

"Damned if I can tell," Captain Delaney said. He was ten yards away in some brush along the stream.

Canyon lay where he had been when he fired. He had seen Long Jack jolt backward into the brush and away from the two army officers. Since he fell into the brush not ten yards in front of Canyon, the Comanchero had remained motionless, waiting for a good shot.

"Hell, he's gone by now, running for good. At least we still have the rifles and his three hundred and fifty in gold." Westcott came in front of his horse and led it forward toward the ten army rifles on the ground.

Long Jack's heavy revolver roared once, then again as fast as he could thumb back the hammer, and Major Winfred Westcott took both .45-caliber slugs in his chest, the second spinning through his heart and stopping the blood pump for all time.

Canyon had out his army issue .44. He was behind the killer's position, so he could see no muzzle flash. He heard the sound but still had no target. Both men remained motionless.

It was to be a waiting game. They both heard Delaney as he ran with his mount away from the scene. There was the faint sound of a rifle stock hitting a man's legs and then curses and quiet conversation.

"Broke my damn leg," Delaney shouted. There was a quiet reply and then silence.

Canyon searched the ground around him, found a fist-sized rock, and decided where to throw it. The spot had to be on this side of the man called Long Jack. Then Canyon could spot the muzzle flash. He threw the rock into some brush ten feet from himself to the side and well behind the gunman.

The rock hit brush and branches and then another rock when it struck the ground.

Long Jack spun around where he lay and fired twice into the spot near where the rock hit. The muzzle flashes were plain to Canyon.

He returned two shots and then rolled six feet to the left. He heard a wail from the gunman. Was it real or fake? He waited.

"Want me to bleed to death, bastard?" Long Jack asked, at last lifting his voice only a little. There was a note of weariness in it.

"Stand up and walk this way with your hands in the air. No tricks or you're one dead Comanchero."

"You know who I am?"

"Enough, move."

"Can't. Caught one of your slugs in the leg. Broke the bone clean in half. Can't walk."

"So crawl this way or I'll put seven rounds from my Spencer right down your gut."

"Hold it, I'm moving. Just don't shoot that carbine. Them damn things should be illegal."

The brush moved. Then there was a rush and more movement, only the Comanchero was running away from Canyon. He snapped two shots from the revolver at the noise, then lunged after him. The wily outdoorsman was out of the brush on the open country, where he wouldn't make any noise.

Canyon fired his last shot in the revolver, then lifted up the Spencer, but the trader didn't return fire and give away his position. No chance to catch him now. Not in the dark and in the open.

Canyon turned back to the big cottonwood and yelled at his backup. "Captain Lancer, he's gone. I'll bring the rifles. You get Delaney?"

"Got him. Westcott dead?"

"As dead as they come. Let's go home."

They came into the side gate of Fort Johnson with Westcott draped over his saddle facedown, Delaney's hands tied to his saddle, and the two bundles of army rifles bound to the saddles behind Canyon and Lancer.

The trooper on Guard Post Number Four bellowed out a call for the corporal of the guard, and six men and the sergeant of the guard came at a trot to Regimental Headquarters.

A minute later the officer of the guard, Lieutenant Emmery, was there to find out what was going on. He saluted O'Grady and stared at the body. "Yes, sir, what's the trouble, sir?"

"I've got a prisoner for you, Lieutenant. Captain Delaney. Put him in a security cell and I want you to stand guard on him until morning. If he gets away, you'll hang. Assign two men to take Major Westcott's body down to the doctor's dead room. Do it now, Lieutenant."

"Yes, sir!"

Lights had come on in the commandant's quarters. A minute later Colonel Colton came out in a robe and stared at Canyon. "What the hell?"

"Damn close to it, Colonel. You have any whiskey in your quarters? I'll trade you an explanation for a drink."

They took Captain Lancer along and went over the night's activity.

"We found the bag of double eagles on Major Westcott. He made the sale, then Long Jack tried to double-cross him and take back the gold and get the rifles as well."

"Lord A'mighty! Westcott. I wouldn't have believed it. Delaney is easily led, but Westcott. I knew his father, a two-star general, retired about ten years ago. This would have killed him, but I think he already passed on. Let's sort it out in the morning."

"One of our two problems solved, Colonel," Canyon said.

"So it is."

Outside, Canyon and Captain Lancer talked on their way to their quarters.

"Those four men still tracking Sergeant Jefferson?" Canyon asked.

"Sure are. Sergeant O'Hallohan is checking them. He wants to nail down Jefferson worse than anybody."

"See you tomorrow at my quarters about ten. Sleep in, Captain. You earned your salary tonight."

15

The next morning, Colonel O'Grady took a report from the corporal who had been following Sergeant Jefferson. He had gone straight from the disciplinary barracks to his own unit and hadn't left all night. He had talked to only two or three of his friends.

That morning all of the noncoms of Able Company met and talked about their loss of a company commander. They were told that a new officer would be assigned to them soon. Until then, the sergeants managed the company. Sergeant Jefferson took part in these discussions.

Sergeant O'Hallohan wanted to be one to trail Jefferson, but Jefferson knew him, so O'Hallohan coordinated the observations.

About four o'clock that same day, Sergeant Jefferson was seen slipping in a door of the stables, and he was not found by the watchers for about ten minutes. Near the same time, Captain Philburton also entered the stable area. Both men emerged about the same time but from different doors.

"Possible that Philburton has something to do with this," Canyon told Captain Lancer. "He was the fourth man in that poker game. Now two of them are dead, one under arrest." They soon set up a continuing watch on Captain Philburton as well.

Nothing happened the rest of the afternoon and early evening. Just after ten o'clock, Jefferson slipped out of his dark barracks and headed for the stables. A runner went to bring Canyon.

At ten-thirty Captain Philburton left his quarters and walked toward the stables. By then Sergeant O'Hallohan had three men planted in the stables waiting and watching.

Both men went into the stables and were seen and trailed by the watchers inside. The pair met in the officers' horse stalls section, and one of the watchers ran out to bring in the others.

Canyon O'Grady frowned as he watched the little drama unfold. He had moved silently in close enough to hear what was being said.

"You messed up, Jefferson. You told me you could kill the colonel, that you were a sharpshooter and could get in the right position so nobody would ever know."

"So he surprised me. Wasn't my fault. This guy O'Hallohan just happened to be in the area. I'll kill him on the next patrol, like I guaranteed."

"Won't be a next time. Too dangerous now. He'll be watching everyone."

"Then we better just both forget it. I won't charge you a thing and you see that I don't get court-martialed."

Captain Philburton scowled and nodded. "I'll try to do that, but it could be hard. They have a witness."

"Sure, but it's not proof; it's just his word against mine, not like he was an officer."

"True, I'll work on it." He looked into the darkness around the stable lantern. "You hear something out there?"

"No."

"I did. Over that way." Captain Philburton pointed into the gloom and Sergeant Jefferson looked that way. He was about to turn around when Philburton slammed the butt of his .44 revolver down hard on the sergeant's head, smashing him to the dirt floor.

Sergeant O'Hallohan started to move, but Canyon put his hand on his shoulder. He held up his fingers skyward, palm toward the trooper in the "stop" signal.

Philburton looked around, picked up the sergeant, and carried him to the side of an area that held ten horses. He draped Jefferson over the side railing, crawled through, and dropped the unconscious man in the pen, then he went to the far side and began to drive the horses toward the trooper, who lay on his back.

"Now," Canyon roared. "Get them both!"

Three troopers advanced on Philburton where he stood trying to push the horses and their heavy shoed hooves over the fallen sergeant. Canyon and O'Hallohan rushed into the horse pen and pulled the unconscious Sergeant Jefferson out of the pen and out of danger.

The troopers brought Captain Philburton around to where Canyon knelt trying to see if Jefferson was still alive. He was.

"This is an outrage, Colonel. Tell these troopers to put away their weapons at once."

"Not a chance, Philburton. So you were the one behind the plot to kill Colonel Colton. Now you and Jefferson both will stand a court-martial for murder."

"I don't know what you're talking about."

"I bet. Probably the whole poker club was in on the plot against the colonel. It'll come out. Unless you want to shoulder the whole blame for the death of that corporal. You and Jefferson killed one of the army's own. For that you should hang. You better have a good lawyer."

"Got no proof. You're bluffing."

"We have five witnesses to your conversation with Sergeant Jefferson. We've got those same five witnesses who saw you try to kill the sergeant by having the horses trample him to death so it would look like an accident.

"Any court-martial I've ever seen would convict you, Philburton. Now, get moving. You have a date with a strong cell and a tough guard."

It was late when they had Philburton locked in a cell and Sergeant Jefferson under the careful hand of Doctor Tabler in the small infirmary.

"He has serious head injuries," the medic said. "I'm not sure if he'll live or not. We'll know in a day or two."

Canyon checked his watch, shrugged at the nearly midnight reading, and went over to the fort commander's residence and knocked.

The door came open almost at once. Colonel Colton stood there, pipe in hand and still dressed. "Had a strange feeling something was happening tonight," he said. "Knew I couldn't sleep. Come in and I'll see if I can find that Tennessee sipping whiskey."

A few minutes later, they settled down in chairs in the living room and lifted glasses. It was good sipping whiskey.

"Found out who the officer was who was after your hide," Canyon said.

"Good. Should I still be worried?"

"Not anymore, at least not from your own men."

The colonel nodded and sipped at his drink. "Guess that means that the two problems are taken care of and we have to talk about the last one, me."

"Not tonight. Plenty of time for that. The officer we grabbed trying to kill Sergeant Jefferson was Captain Lewis Philburton."

"Be damned! I figured he was one of the best officers I had."

"Probably was. He also tried to have you shot. I decided if we cut Jefferson loose, he'd lead us to the men who put him up to the deed. Doubt Philburton was the only officer involved. I'm leaning toward the idea that the whole Westcott poker-party four had a hand in it. Two of the four are dead, and now the other two in custody. A little gentle reasoning with the officers might turn up a lot of things.''

"Oh, I didn't tell you, O'Grady. When we were collecting Major Westcott's personal gear, we found a leather pouch like that other one. It had nearly three hundred and fifty dollars in it in gold dust and gold double eagles. I confiscated it as evidence.''

"Which means Westcott was the other half of the gun-running team. Philburton must have been brought in after Hartsook got killed.''

"Seems like.'' They both worked on the drinks for a minute.

"If Jefferson lives he should be willing to tell us everything he knows,'' Colonel Colton said. "If he doesn't, we have the poker-game four dead or on court-martial, which could mean their hanging.''

"I'd guess the court-martials will take some time,'' Canyon said.

"Told you that you weren't regular army. Case like this can take six months or more. We got two of them.''

"That means I'll have to leave a deposition with the provost marshal, if we have one.''

"Meaning you'll be moving on?''

"Most of my job is done here. All I have to do is bring you that letter tomorrow and have a good long talk. Before that, I'm going to get about ten hours of sleep.'' Canyon got up to go. "Colonel, you should be able to have a good night's sleep now that we have that little matter cleared up.''

"That was the small problem, O'Grady. Now I've got the really big decision to make. Do I stay here and not go out on patrols, or do I call it enough and ask for a transfer to some less rigorous duty?''

Canyon stood, finished the whiskey, and touched his forehead in a salute. "Sir, that's one you'll have to take care of yourself. If the colonel will excuse me, I think I'll become acquainted again with my bed."

When Canyon walked up to the door of his quarters, he saw someone standing in the shadows nearby. His hand dropped to his gun belt and the army-issue .44 whipped out of leather and covered the form. There was a laugh and a woman stepped out of the gloom.

"Been waiting for you colonel, best if we talk inside." The woman was Gert Jones, the officer's handy girl.

"Why can't we talk out here?"

"Too damn many prying eyes. What's the matter, you afraid of me or something?"

Canyon opened the door and stepped aside to let her go in ahead of him.

"Thank you kind sir," Gert said with a giggle.

He closed the door and scratched a match. They were alone, since O'Hallohan had gone to his barracks room long ago. Canyon lit the lamp kept near the front door for convenience. He fit the glass chimney in place, then turned down the wick and put the lamp on the small table.

"Now talk, lass. What is it you want?"

"More than a few things, big man. Most of which have to do with you bare-assed on your bed. First, my ever-lovin' husband sends a message from the troops. Most of them are tickled right down to their socks about how you caught old Major Westcott selling rifles to the Indians. They knew it was happening but couldn't say nothing. Nobody would believe them.

"Now they are laughing up their arses about that damned Captain Philburton. He's been a horse's dick from the first day he came to the post two years ago. Even the men in F Company hated his black heart and the mess he's made of their company. Most of those men been together for more than ten years."

As Gert spoke, she began undoing her blouse and by the time the speech was over, she had bared her torso to the waist.

"My two girls looking for some sexy action, Colonel. A free poking for what you've done for the men and the post."

Canyon fondled her big breasts, teasing the nipples. Slowly he shook his head. "Gert, I'll be honest with you. Tonight I couldn't get him hard if you swallowed him right down to your belly. I'm wrung out like an old dishrag. I'd be sleeping before you got my pants down to my knees."

He bent and kissed each glowing orb and felt their heat.

"No reflection on you or your beautiful girls here. I'm just too pooped to get it hard for you. How about in two or three days, when the pressure eases off around here?"

"Oh, shit! I was planning on a damn long night of lovin'. Hell, it takes two to poke. Guess maybe we better just cool it down for a while. I'm still owing you, Canyon." She started pulling her blouse back on and Canyon leaned away from her big breasts reluctantly.

"Oh, some of the men been asking me if you're really with the IG. They say you don't treat the enlisted like any officer they've ever seen. Hell, you treat them like equals, like real people, instead of jack-boot trash and semislaves like all the other officers do. You for shit sure regular army?"

Canyon laughed. "I'll tell you but you have to promise not to tell even your husband until after I leave. Promise?"

"Yeah, sure."

He showed her his identification card, which had

been sandwiched between two slightly larger tintype photos. The card showed that he was a special agent of the United States government with local, state, and federal police powers, and was signed by the President of the United States, James Buchanan.

Gert handed him the card, her eyes wide.

"Goddamn, you work directly for President Buchanan. Golly! Wait till I tell—"

"Not for a few days. Then tell everybody."

She nodded and hurried out the door, rushing to get home. She'd tell her husband tonight, he was sure.

Canyon carried the lamp into his bedroom and sat it on the dresser. He cupped his hand around the top of the lamp and blew the light out, then fell on the bed. He went to sleep without undressing.

16

It was just after eleven o'clock the next morning when O'Grady and Captain Lancer talked with Captain Philburton in the disciplinary barracks. For fifteen minutes Philburton denied knowing anything about the attempt to kill Colonel Colton.

"Jefferson regained consciousness, Philburton," Canyon said. "I talked with him for about an hour this morning and he gave me names and dates and times and places. He said that the whole thing evidently was hatched during those poker games at Major Westcott's place and that all four of you were in on it. Too bad we can't charge Westcott and Hartsook as well, but they paid the penalty early, I'd say."

"Jefferson is lying, trying to save his skin."

"Always possible. But how could involving you four officers save his skin?"

"I don't know."

"Captain, you give us a complete statement about the conspiracy—how it began, how it worked, the men involved, and the means used to try to kill the colonel—and we'll try to get you a reduced sentence or even reduced charges at your court-martial."

Canyon watched the captain considering it. At last the man sighed.

"Damn. I'm boxed in. No place to run. I don't see what I have to lose. Yeah, get somebody in here who can write fast and I'll spell out the whole goddamned thing. Each one of us was mad at the colonel for a different reason. It just sort of got rolling. Of course, Major Westcott wanted the colonel out of the way so he could take over the fort and sell half of it to the Comancheros.''

They brought in two men with pads of paper and a stack of sharpened pencils and the captain began to talk. It was nearly an hour later when he stopped. By then they knew the whole story of the attempted murder, the death of the corporal who took the colonel to the rear, and the selling of rifles to the Comanchero Long Jack.

The two officers went back to their quarters for a late lunch. Canyon thought through the situation and then, after the meal, went to see Captain Tabler, the regimental doctor.

The medical man shook his head. "Jefferson is hanging on, but there was more damage to the brain than I figured. I don't give him much chance of living more than another day or two.''

"He hasn't been conscious since we brought him in?''

"Not a second. There's too much damage for that.''

Canyon thanked the doctor and went outside. He stretched and looked at the tall Texas sky. Not a cloud. He thought about the lie he had used on Captain Philburton of Jefferson's admission about shooting at the colonel. It had worked, it had pried the truth out of the self-serving captain. A little lie now and then could be a good thing.

He went and found the regiment's legal officer, a Captain Art Campbell.

Canyon told him the situation about needing to leave the post in a day or two. "There isn't much that I can testify to that the others can't cover just as well,'' O'Grady told Campbell. "What there is, I could give a deposition under oath. Would that suffice?''

The legal officer arranged it and Canyon went over those times when he acted alone in the hunt for the gun-runners and the threat against the colonel.

When he was done, the captain thanked him. "I'll have my sergeant write out a clean copy of this for you to read over and sign, then I'll sign it as well, attesting to its authenticity, and it can be presented at the court-martial. It should be ready for you tomorrow morning."

Canyon headed back to his quarters.

Sergeant O'Hallohan wasn't in the kitchen getting supper. Instead, Cindy Lancer was working over a beef stew.

She blew a strand of dark hair out of her eyes and grinned. "I booted your orderly out and told him to take the night off and keep his mouth shut or I'd kill him." Cindy put down the wooden spoon she stirred with and walked over to Canyon and reached up and kissed him. Her arms came around him and she kissed him again. Her breasts pushed hard against his chest and her hips pressed tightly against his.

When the kiss ended, she buried her head against his shoulder and shivered. "Supper is going to have to wait. I can't wait another second." She reached up and kissed him again, massaging his chest with her hands. He could feel the heat radiating from her body. Her breasts burned against him and slowly her hips began to rub against his crotch.

Canyon suddenly wasn't tired anymore. He picked her up and headed for the bedroom. "You're right about supper. It can wait, I don't think I can wait now either."

"Yes, yes!" She kissed him as he carried her, a dozen little kisses on his lips and chin and his neck and his nose. She squirmed in his arms, trying to get her breasts against him.

"Your parents know where you are?" he asked, his voice husky, gravelly with the sudden need for her.

"Yes. I'm at Lieutenant Arlington's having supper with them and working on some delicate stitchery that Lynn Anne is teaching me."

He spread her out on the bed like a rag doll, nuzzling into her breasts, nosing under the fabric. She pulled the blouse open; she had nothing on under it.

"Yes, yes! Suck them, lick them, bite my nipples until I scream. That feels so good."

He did her bidding, first staring at the two perfect hemispheres with their delightful swell and the deep-pink bands around them and tipped by cherry-red nipples, which were already growing and stiffening and rising.

He rubbed the nipples between finger and thumb and she moaned.

"That's so wild. It makes me want to rip my clothes off."

Then he kissed her flattened breasts, working up the sides, darting to the nipples and licking them, then biting them gently and harder until she yowled in pleasure/pain.

She sat up and reached for his crotch. "I want to see him. I'll die right now if I can't kiss him."

She undid his fly and his belt and opened his pants, then found his erection and pulled him out of the short underwear.

For a moment she stared at his manhood. "So glorious! All hot and steamy, long and thick and with a spear-tip point, a wonderful purple head that will drive deep inside me." Cindy shivered. "Oh, God! I can feel him already. I have to be home by ten o'clock. We won't have time for supper."

She bent and kissed the shaft, then moved up to the head and pushed her tongue into the slotted opening there. She kissed down the other side and shivered again, then the song came, a crooning, a soft tune of pleasure and heat and sex and wantonness that she sang like a lullaby.

She pulled his maleness into her mouth and sucked on him a moment, then let him go and quickly undressed him. Her blouse came off in the process, and he marveled at the way her breasts swung and jiggled and bounced as she yanked off his boots, then pulled down his pants and underwear and stripped off his shirt until he was naked.

"Gorgeous! Just simply beautiful." She felt his biceps and his shoulders and the heavily muscled torso and chest, then down to his flat belly. "A work of art, a masterpiece. Oh, damn, but I wish I could keep you forever and ever."

A tear ran down her cheek. He kissed it away, then bent and kissed her breasts again and reached for her skirt.

She grabbed him and rolled him onto the bed and stayed on top of him, humping her hips against him with a sudden passion that left him surprised.

"Oh, damn! Oh, God! So soon. So damn soon . . . so good!" She shivered and then gasped as her whole body stiffened and she bleated out a cry of wonder. "Oh, oh, oh, yes, yes, wonderful! More, Canyon, more. Oh, God! Oh, yes, yes!" She pounded against him with her hips, her fingers clawing at his shoulders and neck and arms. She stiffened again and then dissolved into a series of spasms and vibrations that rattled her like a bolt in a bucket.

Her arms went around his neck and she tried to kiss him, but she shook so much she couldn't. At last the spasms trailed off and she lay there gasping.

Cindy blinked and stared down at him. "Oh, Lord, I did, didn't I? And you haven't even got my skirt off yet." She panted to get back her breath, and as she did, she stripped down her skirt, petticoats, and her softly pink bloomers.

Cindy rolled on her back and pulled him over. She caught his hand and hurried it down to her crotch where she pressed his hand into her moist, super-heated nether lips.

He caressed her softness, then found her small node and stroked it a dozen times, setting her off again on two more series of spasm climaxes. She screeched in joy and roared in satisfaction. Sweat beaded her forehead and she panted like a quarter horse after galloping a half-mile.

Then she eased off, spread her legs, and wrapped them high around him. He stroked her soft nether lips and felt that they were swollen and hot and wet.

"Please, Canyon, push him into me right now. Right now, or I know I'll die and you'll be upset. Fuck me right now, Canyon."

He lifted and moved forward, lowered and moved again, then found the dampness and the soft petals and eased into the slot.

"Oh, wonderful," she crooned. Then the wail came high and long and he heard it go higher as he plunged into her to the end of his stroke and their bodies were lashed together by his marlin spike.

"Glory be. Oh, yes!" Then she moaned in a low voice as if waiting for something.

He stroked and she met him, her body one fluid container all for him, ready and helping. She surged upward to meet him and caught him with her internal muscles and squealed in delight and design, and then she began to build up her own passions. She built and built and he felt her tightening and stroking, and then she seemed to peak and rush over the top.

"Ohhhhhhh, yes, yes, darling! Ohhhhhhhhh God but that's wonderful. Oh, oh, oh, oh, oh. More, more, that's it. Yes, I think that's it . . . ahhhhhhhhhhhhh."

She pushed his pounding hips high in the air, then dropped suddenly and her arms flopped to her sides, her breath sucking in and billowing out in huge gasps to replenish her starved blood cells after the flood of passion.

Canyon had sensed his own heat building as well, but she was far past him and he waited for her; then, when she collapsed, he drilled her with his own need and pounded and she came back, holding him tightly, her legs high on his shoulders, moaning and yelping in time with his furious thrusts.

A dozen hard strokes, then a dozen more, and at last he sensed that the end was near. The gates of the universe opened wide and he jetted into the wilds of outer space, slanting around the sun and the planets and into a far galaxy before drifting back to this world, where he made six hard thrusts, spurting his load deep within her and then dropping on top of her gently as he almost passed out from the orgasm.

They lay there both panting and recuperating. It was five minutes before he looked at her. Cindy's eyes were open and she had been watching him.

"God, that was good," she said softly.

"So good it scares me," Canyon said.

"Do you have to go away?" she asked, moving her hips to relive the joy of the just-past moment.

"I'm afraid so. I've got a boss too, you know."

"But he can't order you around tonight." She kissed him and he felt his hot blood rising again.

"Let's make love once more, and then we'll see if that stew is ever going to be done. We won't waste much time eating. I'm going to make love to you every minute I can while you're still on this post."

Fifteen minutes later they sat naked on the floor of the bedroom on a throw rug and ate bowls of the beef stew and just-baked bread.

"You are fantastic!" She turned and had her hand

formed into a gun, her first finger pointing at him, her thumb straight up. "You are my prisoner. You are under my power. You will not leave in two days. You will stay hidden in my bedroom forever and I'll take you out every night to make delicious, remarkable, wonderful love. We'll be happy forever."

"Fine with me," Canyon said.

Her brows shot up. "Really?"

"But my boss back in Washington might not be quite so thrilled with the idea."

"Him! Is he a general or something? I'll take care of him. I'll take him to bed a couple of times and convince him to let you stay with me."

"He'd probably enjoy that."

Cindy poked him with her spoon. She watched him, serious now. "You really have to go?"

"Yes. Tomorrow I'll have a long talk with Colonel Colton, then the next day Cormac and I will ride out of here heading for the nearest railroad. Somebody said a railroad comes into Austin now."

"Oh, I don't think so. The quartermaster officer would know. He gets supplies as far as possible by train, then by wagon."

They finished the stew and she put the dishes on the dresser. Both of them were still naked.

"Clothes are a nuisance, don't you think?" Cindy asked.

"With a sleek body like yours, they sure cover up a lot of your best features."

"My big tits?"

"That's two good points."

She stuck her tongue out at him. The window was tightly draped and the bedroom door was closed and locked with a heavy bolt.

She bent over him and pushed one breast into his mouth. "Dessert-time, vanilla cake, with a cherry on top."

He chewed on her breast a minute.

"This time I want to do something strange and unusual and wild, like standing on my head or something."

"Sounds like fun. Any workable ideas?"

"No, but I bet you do. I mean you've had more . . . experience than me. You ever been to a whorehouse?"

"Been in a lot of them, but I've never paid."

"What are they like? The women, I mean. How are they different? I mean to sell themselves that way?"

"Most of them are alone, have no other way to make a living. They are just women, no different from other women. I met one once who had been a famous New York society debutante, but she got tired of it, found she enjoyed making love more, and came west to whore."

"Really? Strange."

"How about standing up against the door?"

"I can't do it standing up. It won't work standing up. I'm built wrong."

"Bet that it'll work."

It did.

They made love six times before ten o'clock. Then Cindy dressed and went to the door.

"God, I'm gonna be sore tomorrow, but it was worth it. You don't dare leave without saying good-bye."

"I won't."

She kissed him once more, then looked out the door. She saw no one watching and slipped outside and into the night toward Captain Lancer's quarters.

Canyon grinned as he watched her go. He was going to be sore tomorrow as well.

17

Canyon struggled out of bed the next morning at eight o'clock. When he was shaving, Sergeant O'Hallohan told him breakfast would be ready for him when he was finished. The sergeant had a big grin on his face but said nothing about the night before.

The breakfast was good: bacon, hotcakes, country fried potatoes, coffee, toast, and jam. Canyon wondered what the troops ate for breakfast. No wonder the enlisted men hated all officers.

He dressed carefully so he was entirely regulation, then called in O'Hallohan.

"About last night, Sergeant. That was a private affair. I'd appreciate it if you put it out of your mind. The lady has a reputation to maintain on post. I'm sure you understand."

"Yes, sir. Not a word from me." Still he grinned when he left the room.

At ten, Canyon went to talk to the colonel. They closed the office door and both looked out the window at a company of cavalry going through mounted drill.

"Quite a day yesterday, O'Grady," Colonel Colton said. "I did a lot of thinking last night. I guess there isn't an officer in the army, any army, who doesn't want to get a star on his shoulder. You know I do. You know that's why I got posted here so I could get some Indian fighting on my permanent record."

"You have, Colonel Colton. You have a good record

and it's going to stay that way. Only two of us on post know anything about your blackouts. Captain Lancer is sworn to secrecy, and I'll be a nonentity armywise in a few days."

"You have my undying thanks for that, O'Grady." He looked up. "Is it all right if I don't call you colonel? It irritates me a little to use the term when I know that it's . . . well, it's an honorary title."

"No problem for me at all, sir. In fact, I've thought the same thing from the start. Hell, call me Canyon, that's who I am."

There was a brief flash of a smile and a nod, then Colonel Colton dropped into the big chair behind his desk and scowled.

"Been over all the pros and cons of my alternatives a million times since last night. I can stay here in command and keep up the pressure on the Comanches, but stay on post while doing it. I can ask for a transfer to another post, preferably an administrative one. Or I can stay here and go out on patrols and you'll sack me and I'll be kicked out of the army.

"None of them is what I'd like to do most. I guess you know that."

"Yes, sir. It's a career decision, and that's always a tough one to make."

They sat in silence for a moment. Colonel Colton took out cigars and offered Canyon one. He didn't smoke often, but this was an occasion. They both lit up, sat back in their chairs, and tried to blow smoke rings. At last Colonel Colton got a good one that drifted lazily toward the ceiling, then broke up.

"Well, I decided last night. I woke up the wife and talked it over with her. I think she was pleased, but I'm not sure. Sometimes she can be a strange woman."

They smoked again. The colonel got up and walked around the room, stopped at the window, and saw the troops still on mounted drill.

"The army is going to change in the next year," Colonel Colton said. "Damn big changes. An explosion. There's got to be someplace they can use me in a nonfighting spot. Hell, there'll be as many generals behind the front division troops as there are up there plotting strategy.

"I'm guessing that there should be at least a million and a half men under arms by the northern states within two years. War is coming, maybe within another year. President Buchanan is trying, but he isn't a good-enough negotiator to stop the war. Hell, maybe nobody can stop it. Too many directly opposed forces and ideas and traditions on each side to let it simmer down into a civilian and political struggle. War is coming."

Canyon remained in his chair. He figured it would be a long conference. A thirty-three-year career was in the balance, and there was no reason to rush him.

"Canyon, I've decided definitely that I should not be commanding troops in engagements with the hostiles. From what you tell me, and what Captain Lancer said, I must have some small problem. I know my heart seems to race, my head feels like it's going to explode in those stressful situations. I know you'll have me sacked if I try to go on any more patrols, and I don't want to throw away my career that way.

"Now I realize that some report will have to be put on my permanent records so some general won't drag me out to lead a division in some big engagement—when the war comes, that is. But I'm hoping that the note to my record won't hurt my career in the administrative end of things. After all, that's where I spent eighteen years of my career. You want a drink, Canyon?"

"No, sir. A little early for me."

"Yeah, true. All right, so I'm not leading the contact patrols. I've about decided that I don't want to remain here and direct the fighting long-distance. Just wouldn't seem right to me after I've been out there.

"Which quickly brings us down to the last alternative. I've decided that if it's all right with you and the president, I'll ask for a transfer to some administrative post."

The colonel came back from the window and sat in his chair. "Not what I'd really like to do, but you've convinced me that I could get a whole patrol killed out there against the Comanche if I blacked out at just the wrong time and left the troops on their own. So, what's your reaction?"

"Looks like the best decision, Colonel. Now all we can do is see what the president has to say. He ordered me to give you this envelope after you came to your own decision. Remember, he didn't know what the problem was out here when he wrote this letter."

Canyon took the envelope out of his inside pocket, unwrapped the oiled paper protection, and took the inner envelope out and gave it to the colonel.

It was White House stationery and addressed to the colonel by hand.

Colonel Colton took a penknife and slit the envelope carefully. This one, as well, would be saved and treasured. He pulled out the one sheet of paper and unfolded it, turned to the window light, and read.

Canyon watched him a moment, then stood and slipped out the door. He told the sergeant he was going for a little walk, and to tell Colonel Colton he'd be back in a half-hour. The man should have that much time alone with a letter from the president.

O'Grady walked down officers' row, around the parade grounds, and took—and returned—a few salutes. He could see how a man could get used to this army life. An officer was a superior being in the army. Saluted, obeyed, received special privileges, had many opportunities. Yes, it could be intoxicating. Then there was the challenge of the enemy.

But in the long run he knew he couldn't tolerate the

way the enlisted men were treated. That would change someday, but not for fifty or seventy-five years, he was sure. An army was still an army, not a democracy. It had to be that way.

When he had circled the parade grounds, he came back to the Fourth Cavalry Regiment GHQ and stepped inside.

"Colonel Colton says you should go right in," the sergeant on duty told Canyon.

He went to the door, opened it, and saw Colonel Colton staring out the window again. Was that a bad sign?

Colton turned, a huge smile on his face. He held out a glass of some whiskey-looking drink for Canyon.

"Best damn letter I've ever read in my life. Here, take a look." He thrust the letter at him and grinned. "Goddamn! Goddamn!" Colonel Colton mumbled, but the words had a pleased, almost unbelieving tone to them.

Canyon read the letter.

White House
September 1, 1860

Dear friend James Henry,

I'm not sure what the problem there is, and I don't know how it will be resolved, but when the shouting and thunder calms down, I have a suggestion.

For some time now I've had a vacancy on my White House staff. What I need is a senior military adviser. Sometimes this is a navy man and sometimes an army man. The last one was from the navy and now I'm in need of an army man. The only trouble is that the post calls for at least a one-star general.

I would be pleased if you would accept the post of senior military adviser to me at your earliest convenience. It goes without saying that your promotion to brigadier general goes with the appointment.

If you would care to accept this post, please advise

Canyon O'Grady, and we'll arrange a replacement for you there at Fort Johnson expeditiously.

It's my hope that you'll be able to join our workers here. This position would be for the rest of my term, and then at the pleasure of the new president. However, you will remain on active duty with the army, and your promotion will be a permanent rank. If difficulties come in the future, the star would stand you in the forefront of an expanding military force.

If you need some time to make up your mind, tell Canyon O'Grady. He is a trusted and valued investigator and trouble-shooter for me of three years' standing. Please convey my regards to your family, and I hope to see you soon in Washington.

Sincerely,
James Buchanan,
President of the United States

Canyon O'Grady put down the letter, his own face wreathed now in a smile as well.

"I can see why you're so pleased, General Colton."

Colton looked up quickly at the form of address, then he smiled and chuckled. "A little premature, but I'd say you're right. I'm going to take the post, of course, and get my star."

"Will you need some time to clean up matters here?"

"Yes, a month should be enough. I'd appreciate a replacement by then, and if the army doesn't send one, I'll appoint Major Stanton to take over temporarily until a new commander can be appointed by Division Headquarters. I can leave a deposition for the court-martials. I'm not that much involved."

"If you would put all that in a letter, I'll be glad to hand-carry it to the president. I'll be leaving here for Washington tomorrow morning."

"I'll do it. And tonight there will be a farewell dance and supper for you in my quarters. I'll go tell my wife now to start getting the party ready. At the same time I'll announce my new appointment.''

Canyon nodded and left. He couldn't remember ever seeing a tough old army officer who looked any happier.

Now, to wrap up his own duties and friendships there. First he stopped by at the infirmary. Doctor Tabler came out of the back room and shook his head.

''Sorry. Jefferson didn't make it. He died about half an hour ago. I guess you have a murder charge against that damn Philburton now.''

Canyon swore softly. ''I guess so.'' He thanked the doctor and left.

He went by his quarters and told Sergeant O'Hallohan that he'd be leaving first thing in the morning.

''I want to thank you for all of your help on the investigation, O'Hallohan. I couldn't have done it without you.'' Canyon held out his hand and shook the sergeant's. Then he dug into his wallet and came out with his identification card from between the tintype pictures.

O'Hallohan read it and looked up quickly. ''Damn! This means you work directly for President Buchanan?''

''It does.''

''Golly, that is something. Oh, are you a real colonel, then?''

''O'Hallohan, I've been a colonel for nearly three weeks now, and I don't like it one bit. As of tomorrow morning I'll be plain old Canyon O'Grady again, and glad of it.''

''Good. I mean, I didn't seem to think that you acted like the other officers, you know nasty to the enlisted. Will that ever change?''

''Not in our lifetimes, O'Hallohan. But someday. We just have to make the best of it while we're here.''

''Guess so. Where you headed?''

"Washington, D.C. I'll ride Cormac until I can find a train we both can hitch a ride on."

"That's going to be quite a spell from here."

"I know. I guess tomorrow morning you can go back to your regular-duty assignment."

Canyon got through the colonel's dinner dance that night. Everyone there cheered Colton's move and his promotion.

Canyon danced twice with Cindy. She was the most popular woman on the dance floor.

Both times she swore at him softly, then almost kissed him.

"Tonight?" she asked.

"Not a chance. I have a tough ride tomorrow. This is our good-bye."

"Oh, damn," she said, and grinned. "I'm an army brat and I know that means lots of changes. I'm used to good-byes." She reached up and kissed his cheek and then ran out of the dance.

He was pleased to find no one in his quarters when he arrived just after midnight. He unrolled the civilian clothes he had brought along. By morning the wrinkles would hang out.

The next morning he dressed, found Cormac saddled and fed and waiting for him just outside his door. Canyon shook O'Hallohan's hand, and when he did, he passed a twenty-dollar gold piece to him.

"Thanks, my friend," he said, and rode for Washington. The president was bound to have a new job for him.

"Come on, Cormac, let's show these army lads that a civilian horse can have some style." They pranced out the main gate and headed east. Cormac turned and looked at Canyon a moment, then snorted and settled down into the long ride to the railroad.

KEEP A LOOKOUT!

The following is the opening section from the twelfth novel in the action-packed new Signet Western series CANYON O'GRADY.

CANYON O'GRADY #12

RAILROAD RENEGADES

February 3, 1861 . . . Seven hundred miles from Washington, D.C., to Chicago, and every mile could be a death trap for President James Buchanan unless Canyon O'Grady could put out the fuse set by the deadly Blue Goose Lodge . . .

Major General Rufus Wheeler shook his head at the President of the United States as they both stood in the gently swaying private railroad car that rolled along the sometimes uneven tracks from Washington, D.C., toward Pennsylvania.

"Mr. President, I'm recommending that we bypass this small Pennsylvania town of Bixby and continue on to Lawton for our next stop. You've read the telegram from the sheriff at Bixby. He says he can't guarantee your safety there. He has only three deputies, and one of them is out sick. He expects three hundred people at the station."

President James Buchanan smiled at the three people who faced him. "I know you folks mean well, and you're doing the job I gave you. But we're just getting started on this trip. We haven't been on the rails for three hours yet. If we fail to stop at every town where there are a couple of folks who don't like me, we won't be stopping at any of the towns between here and Chicago.''

"Sir," Canyon O'Grady said from where he leaned against the side of the private car outfitted especially for the president by the railroad. When Buchanan looked at Canyon, he continued. "Mr. President, the telegram said specifically that there were three or four known troublemakers in Bixby and they had sworn that they would, 'Make President Buchanan forever remember this day and the town of Bixby, Pennsylvania.' That is a clear threat, sir. We can't ignore it.''

"Of course not," the president said as he sat down behind a desk that had been bolted to the floor. The chair had rollers on it and he pushed back two feet. He glanced at the only woman in the car.

"Miss Franklin, what do you make of this? Is it a threat or just some good old boys with a few too many beers out to have a fine time?''

Wendy Franklin was a new special agent in service with General Wheeler, and she was frankly nervous and a bit overwhelmed to be working so closely with the president. She hesitated a moment before she spoke.

"Mr. President, I'm not sure. But there is a good chance that it's a bona fide threat. I don't see how we can dismiss it, or worse yet, ignore it. I would recommend that we do not stop at Bixby.''

"Well," the president said, wiping one hand across his forehead and pushing back the snow-white hair that tufted high on his head. James Buchanan was known in Washington as the Bachelor President, and while he had never married, he had a keen and appreciating eye for a pretty girl. He sighed. The weight of nearly four years of the presidency bore down heavily on James Buchanan's frail shoulders. It was the first week in

February, 1861, and this would be his last trip as president. Inauguration of President-elect Abraham Lincoln was coming up March 4, only four weeks away.

Buchanan peaked his fingers in front of his face and looked at each of the people in turn. "I thank you all for your advice, but the decision is up to me. That's why I'm president. We'll stick to the approved schedule and stop at Bixby—unless you can show me some concrete proof that there will be an attempt on my life at that stop." The president paused and looked around.

The three shook their heads.

"Mr. President, we don't have anything that sure. Still—" General Wheeler began.

The president held up his hand. "Then let's stop and enjoy the small town of Bixby. Oh, it's cold out there. Don't forget to bundle up a bit."

The advisers withdrew to the second car of the three-car train. It was made up of the president's private sleeper car, the shorter observation/passenger car with the wide verandalike platform in back from which the president would make his talks, and the engine up front.

General Wheeler looked at Canyon and sighed. "What the hell can we do now?"

"We make sure nobody shoots the president," Canyon said.

The twenty crack army guards lounged in the car's seats, waiting for the next town. They were turned out in new uniforms, polished boots, and well-oiled rifles. Each also had a percussion pistol on a wide leather belt.

"I'll tell the lieutenant that we're stopping," Canyon said. "Wendy and I will get off the front of the president's car the minute it hits the station, and work both sides of the platform. I'll have the lieutenant put his men around the rear of the car to keep the crowd back at least ten yards from the end of the observation car. We'll have the honor guard standing with their rifles at port arms. Wendy and I will work the crowd, mingle in it, and be watching for anyone who looks suspicious. As on the last stop, General, you'll be on the platform with the president.

"I'm sure the sheriff and his deputies will be in the crowd as well. Our big problem is if there is somebody out there who wants to hurt the president, we can't do anything until he makes the first move."

"We should go on through Bixby," Wendy Franklin said. "I just have a feeling about this place." Wendy watched General Wheeler. She was nearly five feet, six inches. Taller than most of the other women she knew. She was slender, with long blond hair and soft brown eyes.

"Feelings won't help us much if somebody starts shooting," Canyon said with a little more bite than he had intended. "Be sure you have that six-gun of yours behind a fold in your skirt so you can get it up in a rush."

"I know my job, O'Grady," Wendy said with a touch of sharpness.

General Wheeler scowled at them. The general was a rather short man alongside Canyon. He stood just five feet, eight inches, and had added a few pounds each decade until he was a well-rounded man.

"Look, you two. We may have fight enough from somebody out there in Bixby. We don't need to do any battling in the ranks. Now stop it."

"Right," Canyon said, and they felt the train start to slow. "I'm forward on the first car," he said, and hurried into the president's car and to the front of it and the doorway where a porter stood ready to open the door and put down a stepping stool. He saw Wendy on the other side ready to get off as well.

Canyon carried two revolvers on this trip. He had the familiar Colt 1860 percussion model .44 in his holster tied low on his right leg. He could fire it five times by cocking the hammer with his thumb between rounds. Then it took him about two minutes to reload the five cylinders one at a time with the linen loads of premeasured powder and ball that had to be rammed into each cylinder from the front.

It took more seconds to put the percussion caps on the nipples at the breach end of the cylinder, again one for each cylinder.

For insurance he now carried a new Smith & Wesson #2 revolver in a belt holster under his jacket. This weapon was only ten inches long and weighed twenty-three ounces. It was a six-round revolver of .32 caliber but had the advantage of using rim-fire solid metallic cartridges that could be reloaded quickly. It didn't have the range or hitting power of the larger weapon, but in close, it was deadly.

Canyon waited for the porter to drop off the car and jumped past him just before the train stopped. There was a crowd on the platform already and it surged forward to the frantic cries of the three sheriff deputies he saw there waving their arms. A light sifting of snow covered everything and the people wore heavy clothing. The temperature was near freezing.

Canyon watched his breath fog in front of him as he pulled his overcoat tighter around him and walked toward the crowd.

The people were curious, men and women, many holding small children so they could say they had seen in person the President of the United States.

Canyon settled the weapon in its side leather and walked toward one of the deputies.

"Keep everybody back ten yards from the president's car," Canyon ordered, and the deputy with the silver star nodded.

The special agent of the U.S. government stared at the town of Bixby, Pennsylvania. The usual stores and shops and the few houses he could see looked normal. They were neat, well-kept and painted. The streets had been cleared of snow, and piles of it showed on the sides and in front of houses.

A man on a horse rode toward the crowd. Canyon tensed, then he saw the man was simply rushing to get to see the president. He slid off his horse, tied it to a rail, and walked forward with the rest of the crowd.

Canyon eased into the throng, working toward the last car, where President Buchanan would be shortly. The mayor of Bixby was climbing to the observation car now, waving and shouting to the crowd. A hush fell on the throng.

Canyon figured there might be two hundred there, total. Not so many to worry about.

The mayor began to talk and welcome the people.

"Luke, get the hell out of the way and let President Buchanan come out," somebody yelled. The mayor waved and motioned to General Wheeler, who nodded, and the president stepped forward and behind a podium that shielded him from the shoulders down.

James Buchanan was a modest-sized man with stark white hair, clean shaven with deep-set eyes and white, thick brows, a prominent nose, and a thin-lipped mouth.

He smiled at the crowd. As usual, he wore a high white collar, white shirt, black suit and vest. He had been a diplomat before he became President, and he looked the role.

"Good morning to all of you fine people of Bixby," the president said. "I'm glad we stopped here so I could talk to you. Thank you for coming out on this cold February morning to see me."

Canyon heard three horses pounding down the hard-packed dirt street. He turned and saw them coming, half a block away. The three men were roughly dressed and one pulled a revolver and fired a shot in the air.

Secret Agent Canyon O'Grady worked through the crowd toward the trio, who kept pounding forward directly at the gathering. They could ride right up to the back of the crowd, Canyon saw with a start. That would put them only forty yards from the president, well in range for a talented man with a good percussion revolver.

Canyon ran then, pushing people aside, rushing toward where the three riders would come in back of the crowd. One of the horsemen lifted a rifle and Canyon had his own Colt six-gun out and fired a shot over the man's head. The rider turned in amazement at Canyon and the rifle discharged into the air. Then he lowered it and Canyon stopped running. He was thirty yards from the men as they rode forward slower now, still too fast.

Canyon fired and his shot hit exactly where he wanted it to, in the charging horse's head between the eyes. The big sorrel went down like it had been hit with a sledgehammer.

Another rifle fired and Canyon turned and looked at the observation train car. General Wheeler dived to his right, slamming his body between the riflemen and President Buchanan.

Canyon didn't have time to find out what happened on the observation car. He lifted his six-gun again and charged toward the three horsemen, one of whom was now scrambling away from his dead mount. Canyon bellowed a warning and charged at the horsemen.